DEATH CRASHES A WEDDING

A PENELOPE STANDING MYSTERY

TESS BAYTREE

CHAPTER 1

*L*ate afternoon sunlight cast a golden glow on the town, creating halos on the pollen-covered cars and sidewalks. Penelope Standing touched her earphones to ensure they would stay in place, so Jake wasn't left on the other end of the phone wondering if she'd slipped and hurt herself. "I'm going to beat your record this time."

"You wish." The hiss of a beer being opened underscored her husband's words. "You'll be lucky to get half the distance."

Holding her phone in one hand, Penelope ran forward three steps, then planted her feet to see how far she could skid in the buildup. She pushed back the strands of gray hair escaping her ponytail and examined the trail she'd left. "Six inches."

"Not bad for an amateur."

Penelope skipped past the argument about whether there was a professional circuit for pollen skidding and, assuming it existed, if it would have an over-50 bracket. Instead, she went straight for the real issue. "At least I didn't cheat by using an incline."

"You have a natural advantage because you don't weigh as

much." The crunch of a tortilla chip was followed by dog paws scrambling over the kitchen floor as Brutus rushed to recover a fallen crumb. Jake grunted, as if the mastiff had lost traction and slid into his legs.

"I have an advantage because I have technique." She crouched to pet the calico cat sunning herself on the Levinsons' driveway. "Don't worry. You have other skills."

Her husband laughed, sending a flash of warmth throughout her body. "I'll let you tell me more about that later."

"After I finish up here," she agreed. "Seth has the rehearsal dinner and probably drinks after that, so the house will be ours." Her grown son was staying in the spare bedroom for the weekend so he could attend a wedding. David, the groom, was a cousin on Seth's father's side.

Penelope gave the cat one last ear rub and then righted herself. Beer meant Jake was already home, and since he hadn't called her from the road... "They didn't have old trail sign-in sheets, did they?"

"Not that far back." Jake's tiny detective agency had been hired to find the subjects of four photographs taken decades earlier. He and Penelope had narrowed down one setting to a specific trail in a national park, but getting more information had been a challenge. "The ranger said he'd check with the guy who retired last year, but he told me not to hold my breath."

"We'll figure something out."

One more turn and then the Art Deco house took up her view. Built in the 1930s, the white house with black and malachite green trim looked like a series of stacked boxes. To one side was a Craftsman bungalow, and on the other was a Victorian cottage; the clash of architectural styles drew the eye.

The famous "Box House" had been turned into a vacation

rental, possibly because nobody wanted to live there more than a week — rumor had it the original owner had prized style over function, so the light fixtures were beautiful in the daytime but cast deep shadows after dark, and the flat roof leaked every time it rained. Penelope had wanted to check out the interior for a while, but not enough to spend the money to rent it for the weekend.

It was a perfect fit for a famous author returning to her hometown for the first time since running away.

Ashley Webb had left before she'd finished high school, and was now a bestselling author of thrillers. Her debut novel involved the scandalous death of a congressional hopeful and the subsequent crime spree of the teenagers involved.

Since a popular politician had died at a local hotel fifteen years ago during the congressional primaries, many people wondered if the novel was really a roman-à-clef. Ashley dealt with the questions by denying everything with a wink.

Penelope headed toward the house. "Have you heard anything about her books? Esther says it's all made up."

"Before my time," Jake pointed out. "But if she was involved in his death, she'd be smart to shut up while she's ahead."

Penelope rolled her eyes. That was what she got for asking Jake, who'd spent a career in law enforcement. "I must know someone who has the dirt. Maybe she'll tell me if I ask her."

"Maybe she'll get drunk at the wedding reception tomorrow and tell everyone," Jake said, his voice on the edge of laughter.

Penelope stuck her tongue out at his picture on her phone's lock screen. Since the bride was related to her ex-husband, Penelope was one of the few people *not* invited to the wedding. It was just as well — even though they'd divorced over twenty years ago, she and Todd could pretend to be civil for no more than fifteen minutes at a time. An entire wedding and reception would be pushing it. "At least Seth will be there to hear it all."

The house drew her eye again, with its odd angles and colors. Even though she knew nothing about decorating, Penelope had always been curious about the interior. "You know... she might want to get to know me before trusting me with her dog."

"If you want to see the inside of the house, just ask." Another crunch, but this time there was no sound from the dog. Jake must have gotten a plate.

"That would be unprofessional." But there had to be *some* way for her to get Ashley to invite her inside.

"I'm not sure your reputation would really take a hit."

The Box House was two doors down from a tiny coffee shop. A familiar gait caught Penelope's attention as a man came out and headed toward a blue sedan parked on the street. "I don't believe it."

"What?"

"I think I just saw Todd." She hadn't seen her ex-husband in person since Seth's college graduation. Todd had given up on the long hair that he thought made him appear younger. Now it was closely cropped, with the gray at his temples giving him a distinguished air. Even his facial hair looked better — a mustache and goatee instead of the soul patch he'd sported for years, though she still thought it looked like an affectation he hoped would impress people who didn't know him. "Dang it. He's aging more gracefully than I would have expected. I thought the horns would be visible by now." As she watched, his car pulled away, headed toward the downtown area.

Jake's voice was carefully neutral. "I'm sure he'll develop some painful, disfiguring disease any day now."

Penelope brightened. "True." She put a hand on her earphones. "Ashley said her interview would take less than an hour. I'll see you soon."

After she hung up, Penelope heard the high pitched barking of a chihuahua. That would be Frodo and the reason Ashley had hired Penelope to walk the dog. Though her latest book wasn't being released for another three months, promotion had already begun, including a remote interview that couldn't be rescheduled. "Frodo can be a little much," Ashley had explained when she'd called. By the time Penelope had finished scheduling the appointment, she understood. Frodo barked when he wanted attention, and he always wanted attention. His yipping made the walls vibrate.

Penelope checked the time. Still ten minutes before Ashley's interview was supposed to start. Maybe the woman was ignoring Frodo because she was busy figuring out the technical aspects — Penelope's video calls inevitably involved rebooting the computer and then calling Seth to find out what the error codes meant. Certainly the noise the dog made wouldn't help the process.

Frodo's barking rang out through the open kitchen window and Penelope hurried toward the door. Even the walkway felt like it belonged to the Art Deco period, connecting the sidewalk perpendicularly to the house, with neat rectangles of evenly cut grass on either side. When Penelope rang the bell, the chihuahua's barks changed tone, getting lower and louder as he trotted toward the door.

Penelope waited.

Frodo continued to bark. Penelope checked the time again. If Ashley had already connected with the interview hosts, she might have put on headphones. Maybe the noise cancellation had muted the sound of the bell. Penelope rang the bell, longer this time, and banged on the door with her knuckles for good measure. With any luck, Ashley would be able to hear her knocking over the ruckus Frodo was making.

After another two minutes, Ashley still hadn't appeared. Penelope checked her schedule. This was definitely the right day — the only reason she'd accepted the job was because Seth was going to be at the rehearsal dinner with the rest of the relatives.

The interview could have started early. If Ashley really *was* trying to talk with Frodo clamoring in the background, she'd be grateful if Penelope went in.

Having come up with a justification to see the inside of the Box House, Penelope put a hand on the door knob. It turned smoothly — no reason to practice her lock picking skills today. Putting her foot in the gap to keep Frodo from running outside, she slipped through the opening. "Ashley? I'm here to take Frodo for a walk."

Then she knelt down in front of the frantic dog. "Hush, you," she murmured. According to the form Ashley had filled out online, Frodo didn't have any food sensitivities. Penelope broke off a sliver of a treat and held it out. "I can't hear myself think with you making all this noise. We'll make sure everything is alright here, then go for a walk." With a prac- ticed move, she scooped up the chihuahua and cradled him against her chest. For the first time since she'd arrived, the house was quiet.

"Ashley?" Penelope walked into the kitchen. "Are you around?"

Aside from the chihuahua vibrating in her arms, the house felt still. Penelope was almost positive nobody was home. This was her chance to take a quick peek. Unprofes- sional, yes, but as long as nobody ever found out...

In the spacious living room, the floor was covered by a dark blue carpet with a geometric design repeating in gold. Bronzed cheetah statues held up the glass table with decanters and tumblers in the corner. Two walls reflected daylight from inverted triangular mirrors, but the bronze cones on the hanging fixtures kept the bulbs from illuminating the darker corners. At nighttime, the room would be gloomy with islands of light. A rounded velvet couch taking up one corner looked stylish, but uncomfortable.

Ashley had only been there less than a day, and Penelope didn't see any sign the author had set foot in the living room.

In the kitchen, a nod to functionality had been made with marble counters, but the black peacock tiles used in the backsplash darkened the room. Frodo's water dish sat next to an empty bowl in front of the sink. A plastic bag of dog food sat on the counter. No special dog treats. Penelope opened the refrigerator. No perishable dog treats either, but there was a bottle of orange juice, a case of bottled water, and — in the tiny freezer — a half-empty bottle of vodka. Penelope looked down at the dog. "At least your mom has her priorities straight."

But where had Ashley gone? Had the interview been canceled, and she'd gone to the rehearsal dinner early, completely forgetting Penelope was coming by?

The geometric carpet continued down the hallway. Gold and blue Art Deco peacock wallpaper in the tiny bathroom made Penelope shudder. Frodo buried his head in her elbow. "Yeah," she agreed, scratching his head. "That's pretty overpowering." All the repeating patterns and straight lines felt too sterile for her taste. Besides, Brutus would knock over the narrow-based furniture without even trying. This was definitely not a house for a mastiff to live in.

The door to the master bedroom stood open, and Penelope finally saw evidence Ashley had been here. Two suitcases were splayed on the floor, nearly empty. The open closet held four dresses still rumpled from travel. On the other side of the chrome-framed bed was another glass-topped desk, this one held up by two chrome sphinxes. An open laptop rested on the surface, with a microphone headset on one side. On the other side, a phone buzzed with the notification of a new message. The screen lit up, showing the home screen icons and a text message too small for Penelope to read.

Unease prickled Penelope's spine. "Where did your mom go in such a hurry that she left her phone?"

The chihuahua whined.

Over the edge of the bed, Penelope could see a chair on its side. If she took three steps, she'd be able to see the floor and assure herself there was nothing there. Ashley could have rescheduled the interview and gone to visit high school friends. People forgot their phones all the time.

Penelope didn't want to look.

"Maybe I should have stayed outside." Jake would have gifted her a weekend in the Box House for her birthday if she'd ever thought to ask. Not that she would have wanted to stay after she'd seen that bathroom, but still. "We could go for a walk now and deal with this when we get back."

Frodo shivered against her ribs.

If she called Jake, he would be over in two minutes. He would tell her to wait outside for him. In fact, he would probably ask why she'd gone inside in the first place. No, he would *definitely* ask why she'd gone inside. She could hear his voice as clearly as if he was standing next to her.

That last bit settled it. Penelope didn't consider herself particularly brave, but she'd be damned if she would let any man tell her what to do. Even if that man didn't know about the conversation he'd just been participating in.

She crossed three golden rectangles on the carpet and stared at the floor next to the bed.

The woman lying on the ground seemed all wrong for the room, the soft curves of her body contrasting with the stark geometric patterns. Her open eyes were already dulled by death.

Ashley had been one year ahead of Seth in school, so Penelope had seen her at all the usual gatherings. She remembered a girl with spiky black hair, denim shorts, and old sweatshirts that hung off one shoulder. This woman had flowing black hair, perfect eyebrows, and carefully lined lips. Her smoky eye makeup matched her author photo.

Except for the brown eyes staring into the void, Ashley could have modeled a scene for "*author in repose*." The eyes... and a crumpled blue silk ribbon draped over her chest. An angry red line ran across her neck. Someone had strangled her.

Whimpering, the chihuahua struggled to get down.

Clutching the dog tightly, Penelope backed out of the room and hurried to the front door. "Oh, Frodo, I'm sorry about your mom," she whispered, trying to keep her voice from shaking.

Frodo buried his head under her arm.

CHAPTER 2

*H*er first call went to the emergency dispatcher, who had a moment of stunned silence when Penelope explained why she was calling. "*Another* one?" Possibly an unfair reaction, but Penelope didn't blame her. Nobody *else* kept finding dead bodies. Then the dispatcher suddenly remembered the call was being recorded. "Can you give me the address?"

"Um..." Penelope couldn't even remember the street name. "It's the weird Box House. The Art Deco one."

"Okay, yeah, I know where that is. I'll send help. Are you in a safe place?"

Was she? She was still in the foyer with all its hard angles and geometric patterns. Frodo quivered in her arms as she looked for his leash. "I think so?"

"Are you still inside? Ms. Standing, how about you go out front and wait for the ambulance to arrive, okay?"

"After I find Frodo's leash."

"Frodo?" The addition of the dog's name had thrown the dispatcher off her script. "Don't worry about the dog. I want to make sure you're safe."

Indignation blew away the cobwebs of shock. "I'm not leaving Frodo here if there's a maniac running around. And if I take him outside without a leash and someone drives up with a siren on, he's liable to run off and get hit by a car." She walked back into the kitchen where Frodo's food and water were. There. On the counter was a thin black leash, just the size for a chihuahua. "Never mind. I found it. I'll go outside now."

The dispatcher cleared her throat. "Okay. Do you want me to stay on the line with you until someone arrives?"

Penelope clipped the leash onto the shivering dog but kept him in her arms. "No, thanks. Have a good day." She hit the red icon to hang up. Jake would want to know.

* * *

JAKE PULLED to the curb and jogged over to her before the paramedics — a tall Black man and a short blond woman — had exited their truck. "You okay?"

Having him there, with his rumpled brown hair and a hoodie covered in Brutus's fur, made Penelope instantly feel better. Her new client might be dead, but at least Jake was with her. "I feel like I should be getting used to this by now."

He moved to hug her, then stopped when Frodo growled. "Fierce little guy."

"Loud, anyway."

The tall paramedic paused with his case in hand. "Do you mind showing us...?"

Penelope led them into the house and back the hall to the bedroom. "She's on the other side," she said, pointing across the bed, then moved away from the doorway to let the paramedics in. They set down their bags and crouched next to the body, murmuring to each other as they worked.

Jake had one arm around Penelope, but she could feel him

looking at their surroundings, ready to push her to safety if a stranger suddenly appeared. He murmured, "If she was already dead when you got here, who let you in?"

"The door was unlocked." At his raised eyebrow, Penelope lifted her chin. "Frodo was barking."

"And you've always wanted to see what the inside of this house looked like." He squeezed her shoulder, then raised his voice. "We're going to go back outside so we don't contaminate the crime scene any more."

The female paramedic looked up. "Right. We'll be out in a few. There's nothing we can do here."

Penelope let Jake prod her back toward the front door, but stopped as they passed the bathroom. "Just look at this wallpaper." She flipped on the light, revealing the repeating blue and gold pattern. Maybe this wasn't the right time to be thinking about interior decorating, but it kept her from picturing the woman lying on the bedroom floor.

Jake inhaled sharply. "That's..." He trailed off. "Please tell me you don't want to redecorate our house like this."

"Not a chance."

"Good. Now stop touching things. Let's go outside."

* * *

BEFORE HE'D RETIRED, Jake had been the acting chief of police for over a year, as the town had searched for a replacement for his former boss. So it wasn't too surprising that half the force still called him "Chief" when they ran into him.

The problem was that Chief Purcell, the current chief of police and the main reason Jake had retired, came to the crime scene with the detectives. By the time his third employee had greeted Jake with some version of "Hey, Chief, it's great to see you!", Purcell was fuming. He stalked into the house, snarling at the officer by the door who handed him disposable booties.

Penelope loathed the current chief. The feeling was mutual. It made for a comfortable relationship, where each knew exactly what to expect from the other.

Detective Brianna Sanchez came to the doorway and signaled to the patrolman tasked with keeping curious neighbors away from the house. Short and thin, with straight black hair that went past her waist on the rare occasions she let it down, Brianna had no trouble assuming control of a crime scene. "Chen! Get a statement from Penelope and then she can get out of here." She ducked back inside before he could acknowledge her.

Officer Chen was a recent addition to the force who looked like he couldn't possibly have graduated high school yet. He gave a nervous glance toward the sidewalk where a crowd was gathering, but followed orders.

Penelope smiled reassuringly. "It's okay. Jake will keep them from getting any closer if it looks like they're going to storm the barricades."

Officer Chen blinked. Jake rubbed his mouth.

Penelope beamed and waited for the policeman to get out his notepad. Then she spelled her name and gave her address and phone number. None of that was needed, of course — Officer Chen could have gotten all that from anyone who had worked there longer than two months — but there was no reason not to help him create a professional report on the first try.

He made an attempt to regain control of the conversation. "You found the body?"

"I did."

"And how did you know the deceased?"

Penelope frowned. "I don't know that I would consider her someone I really know. I mean, she was in the production of *Oklahoma* with my son, Seth, so I saw her when I went to pick him up from rehearsals. Does that count?"

Officer Chen blinked again. "I thought the deceased was an author."

"This was back in high school, before she ran away during her senior year. I don't think she was writing novels then." Penelope stopped. "But maybe she was. Like I said, I didn't really know her back then."

Jake squeezed her shoulder. "Penelope was here to walk Ms. Webb's dog."

Penelope looked down at Frodo, still quivering in her arms. "Oh, right. Yes. That's probably really what you wanted to know. Ashley called me on Wednesday. She wanted to hire me to walk Frodo while she did an interview... Not in person, but with the web camera. Frodo can be really noisy, so she wanted me to take him for a walk while she did the interview."

Officer Chen scribbled notes. "So you took Frodo for a walk and Ms. Webb was dead when you came back?"

"No."

The young man looked more interested. "She *wasn't* dead when you came back?"

"No, I mean I didn't take Frodo for a walk. Ashley was already dead when I got here."

He looked at her, then at the house. "You had a key?"

"No." Penelope glared at Jake, who was staring fixedly at the sky. "When I got here, Frodo was barking. Ashley didn't answer the door, so I let myself in." She stood up straighter. "The front door was unlocked."

Officer Chen nodded, taking extra care to write down what she had said. "And then you... found the victim." He stopped, as if waiting for her to explain the bit in the middle.

"Yes."

His pen stayed poised over the paper. "Behind the bed in the master bedroom."

Penelope eyed him with newfound respect. Officer Chen was made of sterner stuff than she'd expected. "Well, Frodo was barking. So I went inside. I thought maybe the interview had started early. I was just going to grab Frodo and go, but I didn't see his leash. I looked around in the kitchen and the living room. Then I went back down the hall and checked the bathroom and I ended up in the master bedroom and noticed the chair had been knocked over. That was when I found her."

Officer Chen went through her actions twice more. "So the only thing you touched inside was the light switch in the bathroom and the front doorknob?"

Before Penelope could respond, Jake cleared his throat. She looked over at him. "What am I forgetting?"

Jake raised an eyebrow. "Refrigerator?"

"How did you...?" Feeling her cheeks redden, Penelope turned back to the policeman. "I checked out the refrigerator. And the freezer," she added with a glance at her husband. "Orange juice, bottled water, and vodka." She shrugged. "What? I've always wondered how those vacation rentals are stocked. I was curious."

"Of course you were."

Chief Purcell stalked out of the house, straight to her. "Why are you here, Mrs. Wheeler?"

He knew full well she hadn't taken Jake's last name, so Penelope ignored him for three seconds until he was nearly in front of her. "Oh, you were talking to *me*. Sorry." She held Frodo toward him and the chihuahua snarled at Purcell, who took a step back. "I was just giving my statement."

His nostrils flared. "You found the body. Of course you did. I've half a mind to lock you up for breach of peace."

Penelope smiled sweetly. "My attorney's on speed dial, if

you'd like to try. I can't imagine the town council will look fondly on their entire budget being spent on a police harassment settlement."

Purcell's skin turned a deeper shade of red as he stared at her. Then he abruptly walked to his car. "Get her *away* from my crime scene," he yelled, without looking back. The street was quiet as he slammed his sedan's door and accelerated hard.

Penelope frowned at Jake. "I don't think he likes me very much." She sighed. "Do you think he's still holding a grudge about the shoes?" Brutus had vomited onto Purcell's expensive Italian leather shoes at Jake's retirement party. "I *did* offer to replace them."

Jake was still tracking the path of Purcell's car. "We should probably go."

"One problem." Penelope hitched Frodo a little higher. "We need to do something with this guy."

Jake sighed. They both knew animal services was closed at night. "Temporarily," he said firmly.

"Of course." She smiled at him. "Do you think you can get Brianna to bring out his food? I wouldn't want to mess up the crime scene."

CHAPTER 3

$\mathcal{T}$he next morning, Penelope relaxed on the worn linoleum floor of the Episcopal rectory kitchen, an elderly Dalmatian sprawled over her legs and room for her husband at her side. Spot suffered from separation anxiety, so Penelope came over to sit with her every morning while the Reverend CJ Miller held morning services. In return, Penelope got all the coffee and leftover pastries she could handle. "I wonder if they're still planning on having the wedding."

Jake handed her a mug of coffee, then folded himself down next to her and the dog, holding another mug of coffee and a plate with two crullers. "I don't see why not. Ashley wasn't a bridesmaid, was she?" He took a deep drink, set down the mug, and rubbed his face. "We have to find somewhere else for that dog to go."

Penelope hid a grin. Frodo didn't like being left alone. In fact, Frodo barked non-stop unless he was allowed on the bed. But he also growled anytime Jake's arm strayed within six inches of Penelope. Brutus was equal parts fascinated and horrified by the tiny visitor. It had been a long night without a lot of sleep.

"He just needs to get used to you." She tore off a piece of pastry. "You realize there's a good chance one of the wedding guests killed her, right?"

"Not my case, not my problem," he recited in a singsong. Then he turned his head to look at her. "But I don't see why you would assume that."

Penelope frowned. "Ashley comes back to town for the first time since she left and gets murdered. That can't be a coincidence."

"Ah. I see. No, that's probably not a coincidence." Jake shifted his legs so Spot's wagging tail was further away from his groin. "But it could just as easily be someone who wasn't invited to the wedding." He got to his feet, pulled out the drawer stuffed so full of restaurant menus and coupons that it didn't close all the way, and brought it back over to sift through as they talked.

"Emma and David invited everyone they've ever met to this thing. Or Joann did, anyhow." Penelope was exaggerating, but not by much. This was the largest wedding the town had seen in decades and the mother of the bride made sure everyone knew it. Joann had made this her full-time job for over a year.

"Except you." Jake leaned over and kissed her ear. Unfolding a crumpled menu, he smoothed it against his thigh, then paused. "Since when have we had Mongolian barbecue downtown?"

Penelope leaned over to read the restaurant's name. "They closed three years ago." She straightened and broke off a larger piece of the cruller. "I know I didn't kill her. Just as well we weren't invited. Joann always hated me. She probably would have put us at the same table as Todd and wife number three just to torture me. Did I tell you Joann came to my wedding — my starter wedding," she clarified with a smile, "in a long white dress with beads sewn in the bodice? At least five different people mistook her for the bride at the reception." She shook her head. "Granted, most of them were in their eighties and had cataracts, but still. Who does that?"

"People get weird about weddings." He added another menu to the alphabetized stack in his hand and tossed the next to the floor on the other side of Spot.

"True." Penelope rubbed the dog's ear while she thought. "Nobody ever asked me if I saw anyone around the house."

"Still in business?" He held up a pizza coupon. At her nod, he tucked it into his "good" pile. Then he took a sip of coffee and set down the mug, well out of range of Spot's wagging tail. "They were probably too busy trying to figure out why you were looking for her in the refrigerator."

Penelope elbowed her husband. "How did you know I looked in the fridge?"

His laughter turned into a cough. "You *always* look in the refrigerator when you're in someone's kitchen. The very first time you came to my place, I caught you poking around in the freezer."

A smile tugged at Penelope's lips as she remembered that evening. "You had enough condiments that I knew you could cook, and the whole thing wasn't a biohazard. I wanted to make sure you weren't just looking for free domestic help."

"Lord help me if I was." He stopped to open the plastic bag protecting a landscaper's ad, removed the pebbles used to weigh it down, and added the paper to the recycling pile near Spot's shoulder.

"Exactly. I was saving both of us a lot of time." Penelope rested her head on his shoulder and broke off a piece of his cruller. "You turned out to be a pretty good deal."

"You're not so bad yourself." The further down in the

drawer he went, the more outdated the coupons were. The discard stack on the other side of the dog grew.

Penelope reveled in his warmth for almost two full seconds before getting back on track. "But I still think they should have asked me about what I saw. Maybe I have the key to the whole murder."

"*Did* you see anyone?"

"Well, no, but they still should have asked. Or maybe hypnotized me to make me remember better."

Jake stayed suspiciously quiet as he pulled the next flyer from the drawer. Penelope let it slide. Then she remembered what she'd seen before she went into the house. "Except Todd was there. At the coffee shop, but that's right there. Shouldn't he have been at the rehearsal dinner?"

"Maybe it wasn't him. You haven't seen him in a while, have you?"

"Almost a decade. But I'd know that walk anywhere. Though I don't think he knew Ashley, so he probably didn't have a motive. He certainly never helped with *Oklahoma*." She thought about it for a moment. "It would be wrong of me to point the detectives in his direction just because he deserves it, wouldn't it?"

"It would."

"See, I knew you had a good moral compass when you only had two jars of barbecue sauce in the fridge." She sighed and changed the subject. "How is your case going? Any leads on Red-haired Donna?"

Jake's private detective business was off to a slow but steady start. He'd been hired by the executor of a will to find four missing beneficiaries, a task complicated by the fact that the decedent only had first names, forty-year-old nude photos with the faces partially obscured, and the circumstances of their meeting.

"Maybe. Someone messaged me about the post I put in

the knitter's group, saying Donna might be a friend of hers. I'm meeting her in..." He checked the wall clock. "An hour. I have a feeling she may be Donna, but she's trying to make sure I'm not serving a warrant."

"Reasonable." Penelope had spent more than one weekend avoiding the police. "If it's her, you just have one more, right? The woman from the book club."

"Roberta, the woman with no identifying marks who might have once enjoyed Dostoevsky and fresh air," he clarified.

"There can't be *that* many people willing to read depressing literature."

"Keep your fingers crossed. How's your schedule looking today? Lunch in the park?"

Penelope raised her head to give him a sly grin. "Aiming for a bit of fresh air yourself?"

He laughed and kept sorting. "Not with Brutus watching."

"Speaking of dogs... Maybe you should take Brutus and Frodo with you when you meet Donna. Nothing says *harmless* like a man with two ridiculous dogs. And our neighbors might need a break from the noise." They'd left Frodo safely contained in a crate in the kitchen, with Brutus hovering nearby, but Penelope didn't underestimate a chihuahua's ability to bark non-stop. Seth had still been asleep when Penelope and Jake had left, but she didn't think that would have lasted long.

"Maybe I should spend some time tracking down Ashley's relatives to find out what they want to do with the dog." Jake shook his head.

"Good luck. Her father took off when she was in kindergarten, and last I heard, her mother had joined one of those religious groups where you shave your head and travel around on a bus singing at festivals."

Jake inhaled. "You really do store a scary amount of information in that brain."

"And yet nobody asked me if I saw anything yesterday."

After a quick kiss, Jake climbed to his feet. The drawer, now containing just a handful of menus, slid easily into place. He stacked the rest of the paper in the recycling bin, threw out the old bag, and put the pebbles in his pocket. "Try not to add any more dogs to the household until the new one leaves."

Penelope smiled and patted Spot's shoulder. "No promises."

CHAPTER 4

*P*enelope really hadn't planned to interrogate her ex-husband, but she passed the Five Trees Inn and saw the same blue sedan Todd had been driving the evening before. Roma and Juliette — two very sweet pet rats — wouldn't mind waiting a few more minutes for their morning treats. The boutique motel had parking spots right outside the rooms, so Penelope didn't even need to ask which building Todd was in.

The original name of the motel was a biblical reference — Penelope had looked it up once and promptly forgotten what she'd learned — but it had changed hands multiple times since then. The current owners had modified the theme to suggest treehouses and forts. Todd was in the "Moose Lodge", the exterior of which had been painted with streaks of brown like a log cabin, and had the silhouette of an elk. Penelope had asked Herbert, the part-owner and artist, why he hadn't painted a moose instead. "Too big," he'd answered with scorn, and that was that. Penelope respected someone who knew their own limitations.

Todd opened the door on the third knock. "What?" Bare

chested and wearing only thin pajama pants, he was rubbing his face and squinting against the light. The unshaved jawline next to his goatee rasped as he moved his hand. When he figured out who was in front of him, his arm dropped. "Why are *you* here?" Then his head cocked. "Is Seth okay?"

"Seth is fine." Begrudgingly, she gave him points for that concern. Now she had one chance to get the truth out of him. Todd was a fairly good liar, but only when he had a chance to prepare. "I came by to find out why you were at Ashley Webb's house last night."

Todd's eyes opened fully. He grabbed her arm, pulled her into the room, and slammed the door shut. "What is wrong with you?" he hissed. "Are you trying to get me arrested?"

Penelope looked around the room. This was the first time she'd been in one of the units. Herbert had painted reeds and a lake on one wall, and another elk and two hares on another. Perspective wasn't his strong point, so the hares were the same size as the elk, like some monstrous animal deities called upon to protect travelers. Rough wooden shutters covered the windows, and the carpet had been replaced with artificial grass. All in all, it was weird, but not uncomfortable.

In a habit that hadn't changed in thirty years, Todd had strewn his belongings all over, with a higher concentration near the large suitcase that lay open on the unused half of the bed. Penelope frowned at his unshaven face. "Where's Hannah?" When he didn't immediately answer, her shoulders dropped. "Again?"

"We're taking a break." He drew back. "It's not me. I'm not the one who keeps changing."

Now that she'd had decades to think about it, Penelope realized he was absolutely correct, but he still couldn't see what that meant. "That's because you keep marrying women who grow up while you stay the same."

When his hurt look didn't change, she shook her head. "Never mind. Just... next time, find someone who doesn't want kids. Maybe it will take her longer to notice." Being completely exhausted and realizing she had to take care of two people, not just one, had been the breaking point for Penelope. "Now tell me what you were doing at Ashley's house last night."

A veritable panoply of expressions crossed his face, starting with guilt and ending with horror. "I didn't kill her."

"But you were there." She narrowed her eyes in disgust. "What is *wrong* with you?"

"It was nothing! Ashley and I got to talking before the rehearsal started and she invited me over for a drink while she had some interview. Then we were going to drive to the rehearsal dinner together."

"She was in high school with our *son*."

"So? She hasn't been in high school for a long time now. And it was just a drink. Nothing was going to happen."

Penelope closed her eyes and took a deep breath, reminding herself that she was no longer responsible for anything this man did or said. "Never mind. So you went over to the Box House..."

"She didn't answer the door, but she'd sent me a text earlier saying she might be in the shower and she'd leave the door unlocked. So I went inside. And I found her in the bedroom. Just..." He sank down on the bed. "It was horrible, like some scene out of a movie, except I couldn't turn it off."

Indeed, she would have felt some sympathy for him — if he hadn't left and let her discover the same scene. "Why didn't you call the cops?"

Now he looked guilty again. "I didn't want Hannah to find out. Nothing happened, but... She's driving in this afternoon with the baby so we can go to the wedding together."

Penelope shook her head and shuddered. "You really are a

horrible person, you know? You say you two are taking a break, but apparently Hannah doesn't know that yet."

"It's... complicated. We didn't really set any rules."

Penelope had long ago accepted she'd made a mistake with her first marriage, but this cemented it. "You do realize the police are going to read all of Ashley's texts, right? I'm surprised they aren't here yet."

His spine straightened. "No. I deleted them." He looked a little green. "She had it set up to unlock for her face, so I..." He swallowed. "Then I deleted all the messages we sent to each other." His chin rose, defiance lighting up his face. "And it's a good thing I checked, too. Seth sent a bunch of messages. Almost threats."

Tamping down on her instinctive reaction to tell Todd he must have been wrong, Penelope leaned back against the door and regarded him. "Why would Seth threaten Ashley? They hardly knew each other."

"He... I guess he sort of noticed us talking. He yelled at me through texts after I left." Todd's eyes strayed to the fake grass carpet where his shoes lay upturned.

Penelope rubbed at her forehead. "Let me get this straight. You went to the rehearsal, hit on a woman young enough to be your daughter, did it so obviously that your son noticed, and then you drove over to her house, found her dead, unlocked her phone and deleted your texts."

"And Seth's texts, too."

Penelope resisted the urge to roll her eyes. "Oh, well then, that makes it all okay." She shook her head. "You have to tell the police you were there. They're going to figure it out anyway, you know."

Todd put his head in his hands and rested his elbows on his knees. "I know, I know. I just need to talk to Hannah first. I'll tell them later."

Having seen his good intentions forgotten too many

times when the immediate panic was over, Penelope stared down at the top of his head. "You'd better talk to her today. It's not going to take them long to get the record of Ashley's texts. You deleting them just makes it worse."

He lifted his head to look at her. "Aren't you married to the chief of police or something? You can explain it to him, right?"

"He's retired." Penelope pushed herself upright. "Grow up. Talk to your wife — today, before the wedding — and you probably want to get a lawyer before you talk to the police." She opened the door, then turned back to scowl at him. "If Seth gets dragged into this mess because of you, I'll make *sure* you can never have children again."

CHAPTER 5

*R*oma and Juliette had a huge cage full of exercise toys and other enrichment, but Penelope had only ever seen them lounging on the corner hammock. They squeaked at her for being late, then supervised as she cleaned up and gave them fresh food. "Sorry," she said to Roma, who sat on her shoulder nibbling a sprig of parsley as Penelope picked out an array of fruits and vegetables from the refrigerator. "My ex-husband is an idiot." Juliette scratched at her flank in a clear sign of agreement and accepted the peace offering of broccoli.

Todd needed to make a statement to the police. That wasn't in doubt. But Seth might need a lawyer as well. He'd been at the wedding rehearsal, and then later, the rehearsal dinner. With any luck, he'd been doing something with his cousins in the interval between. That would give him a solid alibi, and his father's idiocy wouldn't matter.

Penelope texted Seth to see if he was out of bed yet. She had just enough time to go home and talk to him before taking Heidi, the German shepherd, for her daily run.

Seth texted her back when she was putting Roma and Juliette in their clean cage. *Over at Esther's house. She says hello.*

Penelope smiled. Esther had known Seth since she'd taught him in kindergarten. Seth could never keep the truth from the two of them.

* * *

WHEN PENELOPE ARRIVED at Esther's house, Seth was kneeling in the front garden in a retro t-shirt and jeans, loosening the soil around the annuals with a hand trowel. Esther sat on the path in her wheelchair, laughing at something he'd just told her. She looked exactly like what she was — a retired kindergarten teacher. Some people didn't understand how good that made her at reading and manipulating people. For their own good, of course.

Penelope stayed back a moment, looking at her son. After an awkward phase in his teens, when she'd worried his features would never come together, he'd grown into a handsome young man. She'd even started to appreciate the perpetual five o'clock shadow he called a beard. He had a steady job that paid his bills — in the computer games industry, no less, which meant all that time he'd spent playing online *had* actually been training. More importantly, he'd kept his generous heart and loyalty.

Unlike many of her friends, Penelope didn't particularly pine for a grandchild. When it happened, *if* it happened, she'd be delighted, but she was happy as long as Seth was happy.

But was he?

He'd shown no signs of settling down with anyone. She tried not to be too nosy. Every so often, he mentioned a name, but it was never the same name twice. Caroline, Bobbi (or maybe Bobby — Penelope didn't want to pry), and Viv had all blossomed and blown away like dandelion fluff in the last six months. If that was what he wanted, good for him. Deep down, she worried he'd looked at her relationship with his father and taken that as a sign to stay unattached forever.

Esther looked up and caught her watching. "Grab some lemonade and join us!"

"Thanks." Penelope went up the ramp to the front door, picking up Pirate before the three-legged cat could dart outside. "Behave yourself, sir," she said as she set him down. Then she tossed one of his plastic balls into the living room and he dashed after it. As familiar with Esther's kitchen as her own, Penelope poured a glass of lemonade, threw the ball to distract Pirate again, and went back outside.

"Need me to help with anything?"

Esther, with a lifetime of experience being polite, waved her to the wrought-iron chair next to the house. "Have a seat. We'll watch the younger generation work."

Seth, less tactful, moved the tool caddy as far away from the chair as he could. He'd seen the results of her gardening attempts in the past.

Penelope settled in the chair as Seth turned back to the plants. "How was the rehearsal?"

Seth glanced up, his hazel eyes lit with humor. "You would have loved it. They're using their Australian shepherd as the ring bearer, and she kept trying to herd the flower child. Meanwhile, Joann was insisting they keep restarting from the top and there's like, twenty people who have a role because 'all the relatives need to be involved'. Two hours of complete chaos. Emma and David looked ready to elope."

He laughed and shook his head. "Eventually, the little girl sat down and refused to move, which seemed like the best solution. The officiant had to leave to go to another rehearsal after the first hour, so the actual wedding party got their part done and disappeared. The rest of us were stuck with Emma's mom micromanaging *everything*, which is even more ridiculous when you know..." He stopped and shook his head. "I think the wedding coordinator was ready to chloroform Joann and tie her up in a spare bedroom."

Penelope contrasted that scene with her and Jake's wedding. It had been in the backyard, she'd been wearing a dress she'd discovered at the thrift store, and their biggest problem was trying to keep Brutus from eating everything. An emergency at work meant Jake couldn't make it to the rehearsal, so they'd just decided to wing it on the day. She had no complaints about any part of it. "I'm surprised Joann and Henry didn't have a big vow renewal ceremony. They just hit their thirty-fifth, didn't they? She could have gotten it all out of her system."

Esther raised one finger. "Their anniversary was in January, and Henry threatened to go on a solo sailing trip around the world if he had to attend two ceremonies within six months."

"Henry is a wiser man than I thought." Penelope looked at Seth, who was carefully removing weeds between the flowers. "So, did the rehearsal finish in time for the dinner?" If Seth had gone directly from the delayed rehearsal to the restaurant, he'd have a solid alibi during the time Ashley was murdered.

"I'm not sure." He didn't look up, keeping all his concentration on plucking tiny blades of grass. "We finally realized that having people stick around after their part just made it possible to start over, so after I recited the poem, I snuck out and drove around for a while until it was time to head to the restaurant."

Over Seth's head, Esther and Penelope gazed at each other. Unlike his father, Seth was a *terrible* liar.

Esther broke the silence. "Seth, sweetie, you might as well just tell us what you were doing. You'll feel better." Her tone was the same one she used for five-year-olds in the midst of a meltdown over not having the perfect point on their crayons.

Penelope added, "If it helps, I talked to your father this morning. He admits he went there, but says Ashley was already dead when he went inside. I believe him."

Both Esther and Seth stared at her. Penelope shrugged. "He may be an idiot, but I don't believe he would strangle someone he'd just met. We slept in the same bed for *years* without killing each other."

Seth stabbed the trowel into the ground, narrowly missing a clump of pink flowers. "He *is* an idiot." Rocking back so he was sitting on his heels, he rubbed the bridge of his nose, leaving a smear of dirt. "Hannah is great. And she's pregnant again, which should make him want to pay extra attention to her, you would think. But there he was, flirting with Ashley while everyone else is trying to convince the flower girl that she's doing a great job so we could get through the stupid rehearsal and get out of there."

"Todd claims they're on a break, whatever that means."

Seth nodded. "That's what he told me, too. It would serve him right if she left for good. He doesn't deserve Hannah."

Esther gave Penelope a significant look. Penelope sighed. "So, where did you go?"

Seth looked up, startled. "I didn't kill Ashley."

"Of course you didn't. But I know you sent texts. Did you talk to her in person, too?"

His brow furrowed. "How did you...?" Then he gave a quick shrug, as if nothing Penelope knew surprised him. "As I was grabbing my stuff, I realized they had both left. That was when I texted them both." The corners of his lips tightened. "I know it wasn't Ashley's fault he was going over there, but I thought she should know he was married. Then she replied with some stupid GIF, and I got mad and told her she should... jump off a bridge." He glanced at Esther, abashed. "Or words to that effect."

Penelope suppressed the laughter that threatened to come out at his censoring his language for Esther, who had heard every epithet under the sun. "How did you even have her phone number? You and Ashley didn't keep in touch after she left, did you?"

"Hardly. I don't think she knew my name in high school. But she's on the group chat for the wedding." He rolled his eyes. "The texts are endless."

"Okay, so where did you go after you left the rehearsal?"

He winced. "To the Box House. She'd said she was staying there in one of the group texts."

Penelope *knew* Seth hadn't killed Ashley. Not because he wasn't capable — anyone was capable if they were pushed far enough — but because if he'd done it, he would have stayed, called the police, and confessed. Still... If the police were going to find his prints inside the house, he needed a lawyer right now. "Did you talk to her?"

"No." Seth picked up the trowel again. "I was trying to figure out what to do. I don't know, confront him or something. Maybe dent his car. I hadn't made up my mind."

"But you didn't do anything, did you?" Todd would have mentioned if he and Seth had argued outside the home of the woman he'd just found dead.

"No. I saw Hannah driving away and... I realized that the whole thing was something *they* needed to figure out between them. So I left. I didn't even get out of my car."

Esther nodded. "That's good."

"Yes, but..." Penelope frowned. "Are you *sure* it was Hannah?"

Seth looked up, a more relaxed smile on his face. "Mom, it's not like I could miss her. She looks like a younger version of you with bright red hair. And I recognized her minivan —

the paint's supposed to be red, but it faded to a weird pink color. Plus, it has a 'spicy ginger' bumper sticker. Why?"

Penelope sighed. She'd never met Hannah, but Seth clearly had a soft spot for her, so she couldn't be all bad. "Because Hannah isn't supposed to get into town until this afternoon."

CHAPTER 6

*S*eth was adamant that Hannah wouldn't have killed Ashley. But Penelope knew how she would have felt if she had one small child, was pregnant with a second, and caught her husband setting up a rendezvous with another woman. Though *she* would have aimed her homicidal urges at Todd.

"If you tell the police, they'll arrest her." Even in his agitation, Seth still took the time to clean off the tools and put them away. "She's nearly eight months pregnant."

Penelope held up both hands. "I'm not telling anyone anything. It's hearsay." She let her arms drop. "Or one of those legal terms. But eventually they're going to come looking for you and you'll have to tell them what you saw. Your father..." She couldn't help the eye-roll and head shake. "He deleted the texts between you and Ashley, so it's going to take a little longer, but eventually they're going to get the originals from the big computer in the sky."

"The cloud, Mom."

"Whatever. My point is that you'll have to tell the truth. If Hannah didn't do it, there won't be any trace of her in the house. And if she *did* do it, keeping quiet about her being there isn't helping anyone, least of all you."

"I know." He stood up. "I need to get going. I'm supposed to meet David and the groomsmen on the golf course in thirty minutes." He went off to stow the tools in the shed.

Esther spoke quietly. "Give him some time to think about it. He'll figure it out."

Penelope took a deep breath and shook her head. "I could *kill* his father."

Esther raised an eyebrow. "It's a good thing my hearing isn't very sensitive these days."

When Seth came back, he kissed Penelope and Esther on their cheeks. "I'll come by again tomorrow before I leave," he told Esther.

Penelope sat up. "If you're going to the house and the dogs are there, can you let them out back for a few minutes?"

"I think Jake took them with him, but I'll check." He started down the sidewalk.

Penelope thought of another question. "Seth! What was Ashley doing at the wedding?"

Her son pivoted and came back, an odd look on his face. "That's the thing. She was reading something, but I'm not sure what."

"You didn't hear it during the rehearsal?"

He winced. Then he took two steps toward them and lowered his voice. "If I tell you something, you have to promise not to say anything about it for at least..." He checked his phone. "Nine hours."

"Except to Jake," Penelope promised. Esther nodded.

Seth took a deep breath and looked faintly guilty. "Emma's mom kept adding more and more to the wedding. Totally out of control."

"Honey, that's not a secret."

"Right, but Emma and David were talking about just

calling the whole thing off and going to Vegas. That's when Joann told Emma that she had cancer and the doctors said she only had six months, and she didn't want anybody to know. She just wanted to do this one last thing."

Penelope and Esther exchanged a look. Esther raised her brows. "She looked the picture of health the last time I saw her at the pool. Not that people don't hide things well, but..."

Glancing around, Seth dropped his voice again. "That's the thing. Emma found out it was all a lie. Joann just wanted to make all the wedding decisions."

Penelope glanced at Esther. "How could she possibly hope to get away with that?"

Esther shook her head. "Miracle cure? Or maybe a new round of 'tests' that shows it wasn't cancer after all."

Seth shrugged. "I don't know. When they found out she was lying, Emma and David wanted to cancel the whole thing. But Henry convinced them to just change a few things without telling her."

Esther sat back in her chair. "Oh boy."

"Joann thinks I'm reciting 'I Carry Your Heart' by E. E. Cummings."

Penelope's days of reading poetry were long past, but she'd heard that one at a recent wedding. It was romantic and short and even an ignoramus like her could understand the gist of it. "And what are you really reciting?"

His cheeks reddened. "One of his erotic poems." He ducked his head. "I only agreed to it because I knew you wouldn't be there. That would have made it weird."

Esther barked in laughter, one hand coming up to cover her mouth. Penelope made a note to look up what erotic poems E. E. Cummings had written. Maybe she could get into poetry after all.

Seth smiled, still embarrassed. "And it wasn't just me. Claudia is supposed to be singing 'Can't Help Falling in Love', but she's really singing 'Genie in a Bottle'. She even has the harpist on board."

Penelope blinked. "Joann is going to burn down the church."

Esther shook her head. "No, she would never interrupt the ceremony."

Seth nodded. "That's what Emma says. So she and David have planned this ceremony that is actually going to be kind of over the top and fun *and* she gets to stick it to her mom at the same time."

Penelope thought about her original question. "So you have no idea what Ashley was going to read?"

"No. I don't think anybody did. David asked her a couple times, but she just laughed. During the rehearsal she read an allegory she had written about two trees growing side by side, but I think she had something else for the actual wedding." He shook his head slowly. "She laughed and said it had all happened when they were teenagers and people would be shocked."

* * *

PENELOPE STAYED in the front yard, sipping lemonade with Esther after Seth had gone. A quiet breeze made the tree leaves dance, showering them with pollen. "Chief Purcell is going to have a field day when he finds out Seth and Todd and Hannah were all in the area."

"The sheer volume of suspects might be the only thing that slows him down," Esther agreed. "I wonder what she was planning to read." She shook her head. "Ashley was a bright child. Loyal to a fault. But no sense of self-preservation, even as a five-year-old. On her own, she would never get into trouble. But if her friends were doing something they shouldn't..." Esther shrugged. "She wasn't the type who would tell an adult or even just refuse to go along. So she, Lenz, and Kieran were always getting into something."

Penelope watched the dappled sunlight move across the flowers. "I never met Lenz and Kieran. Ashley was older than Seth and they ran in different crowds."

"Lenz and Kieran didn't go to the public high school. Something happened the summer before their freshman year — I never got the details. Their parents split them up after that. Lenz was home schooled. Kieran went to St. Luke's." And Ashley went to the public high school with Seth. "Whatever the reason, it seems to have worked; they've all done well in life. Ashley had a bestselling novel. Lenz became a journalist. He's with Channel 8 now — I'd be surprised if he doesn't get called up to the national news soon."

"Wait, Lenz Russell? The guy with the cowlick who's always doing the interviews after every disaster?" Penelope had seen him interview a family describing a fountain of raw sewage erupting in their home after a collapsed pipe. Despite her antipathy toward television journalists in general, she'd been reluctantly impressed at his gravitas while the homeowner reenacted the scene.

"Yes. He reads his scripts articulately when he's in the studio. I'd like to think I had a hand in that." Esther brushed pollen from the arm of her wheelchair. "And Kieran's likely to end up in the state assembly after the next election."

Penelope nodded. Kieran Engle had a young politician's ability to come up with five-second quotes that went viral on a regular basis. He was also David's best man, a fact that Joann inserted into any conversation she could. "You've read Ashley's novel. Do you think there could be any truth to it? If she was going to name names in the middle of the wedding, someone may have had a motive to kill her." Someone other than Seth, his father, or his father's current wife, she meant.

Esther stared into the distance as she thought. "I would

have said not. The events of the novel fit the basic facts well enough — a politician died here during the primaries. What was his name? I want to say it was something like Michael Plum or Mustard or something like that."

"Mathew Scarlet." Penelope remembered all the *Take a Stand with Scarlet!* campaign posters slowly disintegrating after his campaign had come to its abrupt end.

"Ah, yes, another name from Clue. But in the *book*, the politician is in bed with two teenagers, a boy and a girl, when things go wrong and he suffocates. The description is just kinky enough to make sure people talk about it, without being so explicit it turns people off. But I really don't think it's based in reality. If that had happened in real life, there would have been rumors. You know as well as I do how kids tell secrets."

Penelope nodded. Pregnancies, drug use, even attempts at self-harm — it all got around the high school within days. Esther was right. If two teens had been involved, at least one of them would have talked. Except... "How long after that did Ashley run away? I've never connected the two events before, but that might explain why there weren't rumors."

"I'm not sure. I guess it's possible." Esther sipped her drink.

Penelope felt Esther's doubts from six feet away. "I'm not sure I buy it, either. If Ashley came out and said it was all true, she could be charged with something. Manslaughter, at least."

"Unless it's past the statute of limitations."

Penelope made a face. She hated trying to remember stuff like that. But Jake would know. She'd ask him later.

CHAPTER 7

*O*n her way to her next client, Penelope stopped to lean against the huge cork oak tree by the elementary school so she could check her mail. She'd tripped on the uneven sidewalks enough times to know that staring at her phone and walking was a bad idea. A sprained ankle — or worse — wasn't on her list of fun reasons to sit around during the day.

There were no messages from clients, but Seth had sent her a list of links. *This should save you some time.* Penelope squinted at the tiny text. Seth had compiled a list of Ashley's social media accounts.

She tapped on the first link and scrolled through the entries. Ashley's desk in a corner of her apartment. A close-up of Frodo on a sidewalk. Frodo snoozing in his bed. A plate of food, with Chinese takeout cartons visible in the background. Selfies in front of her laptop in the park. The lotions and creams of her nightly skin care routine. Selfies in a different park.

Penelope went to the next link Seth had sent. That platform encouraged brief text, but it was mostly talk of how productive Ashley's day had been, complaints of food delivery waiting times, or observations concerning Frodo. On another site, Ashley interacted with other authors, talking about locations they liked to write at, and conferences they were planning to meet up at. There was no sense that she interacted with any of them in her daily life.

The only people in recent posts other than Ashley were her agent and her dog walker. In both cases, the pictures were group selfies, at various restaurants with her agent and near her apartment's front door with her dog walker.

Perhaps the dead woman had carefully curated her social media to avoid revealing personal information. Though if she had, she'd missed some important clues. The address of her favorite Chinese restaurant was clearly visible in one picture, and Penelope could see distinctive architecture through Ashley's window — if Penelope had lived in the same city, she would have had no problem determining the writer's home address.

The more likely answer was that there wasn't anything to reveal. From the various photos, Penelope would have bet money that Ashley lived alone in her apartment. Food for one, evenings and weekends with the dog... It really didn't look like Ashley's private life was the kind that inspired homicidal thoughts. True, anything was possible, but after spending five minutes looking through the author's life, Penelope thought the cause for her murder was more likely to be found here, not in New York.

What had she been planning to read at the wedding?

Penelope needed to find out who killed Ashley before the police settled on Seth.

* * *

THREE HOURS LATER, the smell of freshly mown park grass competed with the aroma of fast food, providing the perfect scent of the outdoors. Penelope breathed in deeply.

"You were right," Jake said as he handed her both leashes. They walked across the grass to the vacant picnic benches next to the playground. Frodo pranced along in front, with Brutus stalking the smaller dog from the rear.

"Of course I was." Penelope detoured around a gopher hole. "About what?"

"About appearing harmless with the dogs. Or maybe she was just too distracted by the odd couple to worry about me."

"And was it Donna?"

"Birthmark and all." He made a production of opening the bags, spreading out French fries, and figuring out which cheeseburger was hers.

Penelope narrowed her eyes at him. "That birthmark wasn't exactly easy to see if she had a shirt on."

Jake's lips twitched. "Donna is a woman of remarkably few inhibitions." He dipped a fry in ketchup. "You would like her. She's a painter. Refreshingly direct."

"Uh huh." Penelope settled on the bench next to him. "You got a child's burger for Frodo."

"It would be rude to feed Brutus and not get anything for the visiting dog. And he just lost his owner."

Penelope leaned over to kiss his cheek, then wiped off a smear of ketchup. "Have I ever told you how much I love you?"

"You might have mentioned it once or twice, but my memory's going to start failing soon. You should probably repeat it every once in a while." He put a large burger down in front of Brutus, and a wedge of the kid's burger in front of Frodo. "How has your day been?"

"Educational. Did you know E. E. Cummings wrote erotic poetry?"

"Did he? Freshman English would have been bearable if I had." He went back to his own food. "And was it Roma and Juliette who clued you in, or is Esther trying to get you to join her book club again?"

"Esther has accepted me for the philistine that I am. No, it was Seth, actually." She told him of the wedding fiasco and the plan to switch all the expected performances. "I promised not to say anything until after the wedding, but I guess it might be worth mentioning it to Detective Sanchez." Penelope rolled her eyes and stabbed a fry into the pool of ketchup. "Seth shows every sign of throwing himself in front of a bullet to protect the pregnant lady. But if Hannah can deal with Todd and a small child at the same time, she's a lot stronger than Seth is giving her credit for."

While Jake continued eating, Penelope told him what she'd learned from Todd and Seth. On the grass, Brutus leaned toward Frodo, who was picking at his chunk of hamburger. The chihuahua responded with a snarl that had the mastiff backing to the end of the leash. Penelope took pity on the mastiff and tossed him the rest of the kid's burger.

Jake listened in silence. After she finished speaking, he carefully wiped his fingers off on a flimsy napkin. "I'd say you have terrible taste in men, but that would be self-incriminating."

"Let's just say I've learned from my mistakes."

Jake sighed. "Todd needs to give a statement. I'll talk to Brianna and see if she can drop by the house to talk to Seth tomorrow. There's probably no reason to make them miss the wedding." He fought back a smile. "I don't want to give Joann someone else to blame for the whole thing."

"That may be important." Penelope ate the last fry and balled up the trash. "Do you need me to take the dogs home?"

Reaching for the leashes, Jake shook his head. "I have the

time. I'm going to go back over all the paperwork for the missing models. Hopefully, I missed something, because otherwise I don't know how I'm going to track down Roberta."

"You'll figure out something." Penelope tossed the trash at the trash can, then got up to retrieve it when she missed. "It would have been a three-pointer if I'd made it from that distance. Maybe even more than three points."

"No comment." When Jake stood, the dogs sprang to their feet. "Do you need help with anything this afternoon?"

"No," Penelope answered absently as she watched a reddish-pink minivan pull up to the curb near the play structures. Seth was right — that van could be easily identified. She blinked and turned her focus back to Jake. "You could take care of Tinkerbell for me," she said with a smile. Tinkerbell was a Rottweiler who disliked men.

Jake took an involuntary step back and held up his hands. "She's all yours."

"That's okay. I only have a few appointments. I should even have time to make a stop at the library."

He waggled his brows. "Picking up a book of poetry?"

She laughed. "That's not a bad idea. But I thought I'd see if they have a copy of Ashley's novel, the one that caused all the fuss. Maybe I'll find something interesting."

Jake enveloped her in a hug. "Or maybe you should let Brianna handle the investigation," he murmured, but he said it without conviction.

"I will, I will." She leaned forward to kiss him. "I just need to meet someone first. See you tonight."

CHAPTER 8

ased on the van and Seth's description of his father's current wife as a pregnant red-haired woman with a small child, Penelope wasn't surprised to find that the minivan she'd seen parking near the play structures had a bumper sticker with a mermaid's body and flowing locks that created the words 'spicy ginger'. She walked across the grass to the bench where the younger woman with auburn hair watched a blond toddler dig in the sand. Hannah rubbed her belly absently. From the size of the bump, she had to be at least seven months along.

Suddenly unsure of herself, Penelope stopped five feet away and gave a sharp wave. "Hannah? You *are* Hannah, right?"

The woman looked up with an uncertain smile, the expression of someone who has spent her life perfecting the art of always being pleasant. But Penelope could see a hint of tears pooling above her lower lids. "Hi! Have we met...?" Then her eyes widened. "I know you! You're Seth's mom!"

"Penelope." She gestured to the minivan. "Seth described your car and you and I just wanted to introduce myself."

"Sit, sit!" Hannah patted the bench next to her, then winced. "Oh, sorry, I sound like I'm talking to a dog, don't I?"

Only a poor trainer would repeat a command like that to a dog. Penelope kept that thought to herself and took a seat. "Seth tells me good things about you." She looked down at Hannah's abdomen. "Congratulations! How are you feeling?"

Hannah gave a watery laugh. "Oh, you know. My ankles are swollen, I can't tie my own shoes, and every time I try to sleep, she punches me in the kidney. Plus, my hormones are all over the place. But she just has to stay in there for another six weeks. Then at least I won't have to pee every five minutes."

Penelope remembered the last month of her pregnancy. "I think I only got through it because I didn't know what was coming. You're a brave woman for having a second."

"It's not all bad." Hannah rubbed her belly again. "I kind of enjoy feeling her move around when I'm already awake. If it were up to me, I'd probably have a bunch more."

Penelope tried not to react. From what Todd had said, this marriage might have already gone the way of his first two. "You're in town for Emma and David's wedding?"

"Yes. Todd drove down yesterday for the rehearsal, but I didn't want to mess up Charlotte's routine, so I stayed home last night." The words came out in a monotone, as if she were reciting a story they'd agreed upon.

"Ah." Penelope waited a moment in silence as she tried to figure out the best approach. "Hannah, you know Ashley Webb was murdered last night, right?"

Hannah nodded, tears back in her eyes.

Penelope kept her voice gentle. "Seth saw your car outside the house."

"Oh." The younger woman's lower lip trembled. "Oh, Penelope, it's all such a mess. I don't know what to do. And I'm the person who *always* figures out what to do."

Because Todd can't be bothered, Penelope thought uncharitably. She reached over to rub Hannah's back, even as she made a list. "We'll get you a good lawyer — Jake knows them all — and we'll make sure the police don't do anything until Monday, so you don't have to wait in jail over the weekend to be arraigned. Jake and I and Seth can help take care of Charlotte, so don't you worry about that..." She trailed off at Hannah's baffled look. "Hang on. You didn't kill Ashley."

Hannah blew out a breath somewhere between a laugh and a sob. "No. Though I can't say I didn't think about it when I was driving yesterday."

"How did you even find out?" After blurting the words, Penelope winced. Not exactly the most delicate question she'd ever asked, and she had a long history of putting her foot in her mouth.

Hannah didn't seem to notice. "Todd's texts also go to his computer, and I always keep an eye on them. He has a habit of forgetting he's agreed to things. And I have to monitor the wedding chat because Joann keeps changing things around." She shook her head and her voice steadied. "I'm surprised Emma and David haven't just eloped."

"That's a surprisingly popular opinion," Penelope murmured.

Hannah huffed a laugh. "Joann is the worst." She took a long, shaky breath. "So I saw the text when Ashley sent Todd her address, and... Todd and I have been going through a rough patch lately, and we decided he would stay at the motel here for a few days so we'd both have some time to think about what we wanted."

Penelope gritted her teeth and kept her mouth shut. It was completely on brand for Todd that during this separation to think about things, he got to stay in a motel and have someone else cook and clean for him, and Hannah was stuck at home with the toddler.

"I loaded up Charlotte in the van and we drove down. I'm not sure what I was going to do. There really wasn't a plan. But then I got to the house and realized I should have found a sitter for Charlotte. I couldn't have it out with Todd when our daughter was right there, and I couldn't leave her alone in the car." She shook her head. "My brain is mush these days."

"Probably because you haven't slept more than two hours at a time for a couple years," Penelope suggested. "It gets better. Eventually."

"When I saw Todd go into the house, I started crying. Then someone knocked on the window to make sure I was okay. I recognized him. It was that guy from Channel 8, the one with the weird haircut who's always sticking a microphone in someone's face and saying 'And how did watching your whole family get killed make you feel?'."

"Lenz Russell?"

"Yes! He always has that one lock of hair that's always sticking up. Drives me crazy when I'm watching the news. If he stopped getting his hair cut at a chain and went to someone with more experience, it would look better." She sat up straighter. "I used to cut hair before I had Charlotte." She sighed. "Anyhow, seeing him made me realize how stupid I was being. So I drove home. After I stopped at the diner to pee. Again."

In the play area, Charlotte threw a handful of sand in the air. It blew back into her face and she blinked a few times, then wailed.

Hannah levered herself to her feet. "I need to get her back to the motel so she can take a nap before the wedding. It was really nice to meet you, Penelope." A giggle bubbled out of her, and for the first time, Penelope thought she was seeing what Hannah might look like when she was well rested and happy. "You were ready to set up a whole defense strategy for a stranger."

"Pregnancy should be an extenuating circumstance for most things," Penelope replied. She found herself liking this younger woman. "Let me give you my number. Call if you need to talk. And if you need someone to watch Charlotte while you're in town, either Seth or I can work it into the schedule."

CHAPTER 9

*a*n emergency appointment to help clean up a terrier who'd been sprayed by a skunk left Penelope in need of a wardrobe change. She sniffed at her shirt and changed her mind about going through the front door. Brutus was reasonably well behaved, but exciting smells occasionally short-circuited his brain, and the dog weighed almost as much as she did. Instead, she went through the side door into the garage, peeling off her t-shirt and sweatpants and starting a load of laundry.

In her sports bra, underwear, socks, and tennis shoes, she went into the kitchen. Brutus met her at the door, investigating her stomach with delight. "Yeah, your buddy Rocky got skunked again," she told him. "He needs to learn to leave the stripey cats alone." Brutus pushed his nose into her abdomen and inhaled deeply.

Frodo trotted around the corner, his nails clicking against the linoleum. Penelope leaned over to pet him and let him check her hands. "Yes, this is a fun smell, isn't it?"

When she stood up, she found Jake in the kitchen. And he wasn't alone. A familiar face with its equally familiar cowlick sticking up from his head stared back at her. "You're Lenz Russell!"

The reporter blinked. "Yes. Nice to meet you."

Jake cleared his throat. "We were just going to the office to discuss what Lenz needed a private investigator for. Care to join us?"

Penelope grinned at him. Leave it to Jake to act like there was nothing unusual going on. "Let me take a quick shower to get rid of the skunk odor, and I'll be right down."

"Of course. We'll get all the paperwork out of the way first." Jake winked at her as he guided Lenz away.

When Penelope came down the steps ten minutes later, fully dressed and with both dogs at her heels, she found the men seated around the desk in the office. "What'd I miss?" she asked as she dropped into the third chair.

Jake looked up from his notes. "Mr. Russell is in the running for a position with a national news organization —"

"It's a secret," Lenz cut in. "My producer can't know about this until I have a signed offer."

Jake nodded and continued. "And someone is threatening to publicize photos that will cause him some embarrassment unless he pays them."

Penelope raised her eyebrows. "Blackmail?" Then she reconsidered. "Or is that extortion? I get the two confused."

"Blackmail," Jake confirmed.

Penelope looked at Lenz. "Do you know who's doing it?"

"No." A frown flashed across his features. "I thought I did, but... I was wrong."

Jake wrote something in his notebook. "And the context of the pictures?" When Lenz didn't reply, he put down his pen. "I don't need specifics, but I do need to know if anyone else is in them and who else would have known."

"That's the thing," the reporter said, his voice calm. "The other person in the pictures died a long time ago. But if those photos come out, my career will be finished." He looked back and forth between them. "Everything I say to you is privileged, right?"

"Unless I'm subpoenaed," Jake said.

Lenz took a long breath. "Senior year of high school, Ashley Webb, Kieran Engle, and I sometimes went out together. We all had fake IDs, and it was a game to see where we could go. Kieran was into politics even then, so he always picked high end hotels, where we could have some drinks and listen to the deals being made around us. Kieran and Ashley were together, off and on, and he used other men flirting with her as a way to meet powerful people."

Clearly, their parents hadn't been as successful at breaking up the trio as they'd thought. Penelope had an idea of where this was going. "Mathew Scarlet."

Lenz nodded. "We went out together one night, to a hotel bar. The usual thing, with a bunch of boring people talking about things I didn't care about. Ashley and Kieran got in a fight, and Kieran left. And that was when Mathew Scarlet came over." He glanced at Penelope in embarrassment. "He talked to us, mostly Ashley, for a while and then eventually he invited..." He trailed off.

Jake sounded matter of fact. "He invited Ashley up to his room."

"He invited *both* of us up to his room," Lenz corrected. "To play poker. Mathew and I were playing for money. Ashley was broke, so she was playing strip poker." He shrugged. "We were in a bar, so Mathew assumed we were at least twenty-one. Ashley thought the idea was hilarious. So we went to his room and played for a couple of hours. Ashley was a decent player — I'd lost all my money and Mathew lost a pair of cufflinks by the time she took her shirt off. She could have used her winnings to bet with, but she wanted the money. At about midnight, Mathew said he had to get some sleep. So we left."

Lenz frowned as he continued. "All that other stuff, the bondage and everything else I heard Ashley put in her book, that was all made up. Mathew Scarlet was alive and well when we left. Ashley even tried to give his cufflinks back, but he said she won them fair and square. She used what she won to buy a bus ticket to New York that weekend."

Since Lenz seemed more comfortable telling all this to Jake, Penelope dug her fingers into the chair cushion and kept quiet. Jake glanced at her and the corners of his mouth twitched before he turned his attention back to Lenz. "But there were pictures."

Lenz winced and smoothed a hand over his hair. The cowlick popped right back up. "Ashley took a couple with her phone."

"Did Mathew Scarlet know?"

"No. *I* didn't even know she'd taken them until we were leaving the hotel. And I always assumed she'd deleted them the next morning when we heard he had died." He shook his head. "I was only eighteen, but... You don't understand how paranoid the networks are. They expect their on-air person-alities to be squeaky clean. If the photos get out, I'll be lucky to get a job in a convenience store."

He was right about that, Penelope reflected. If Mathew Scarlet was visible in any of the photos, even the people who assumed Ashley's novel was pure fiction might change their minds. And with Ashley dead as well, nobody other than Lenz could argue that it wasn't true.

But if Lenz thought Ashley was the one blackmailing him, he had a great motive to murder her.

Jake leaned back in his chair. "Did you talk to Ashley?"

The perfectly controlled reporter facade was back. "Not in person. She swore it wasn't her. She said her phone had been stolen in New York and whoever ended up with it must have recognized one of us and put it together with what happened in her book."

"And you believed her?"

"Yes." He paused. "No." That word was drawn out, as if he wasn't sure. "I can believe she kept the photos, but anonymous blackmail? Why not call me up and ask to borrow money if she needed it? Besides, they're making a movie from the novel — I think she was banking more money than I was. But I hadn't had any contact with her for over a decade, and people change..." He shrugged. "Then someone put another note in my mailbox this morning. So it couldn't have been her."

"Or she had an accomplice," Jake pointed out. "If she had sent the pictures to someone the night she took them, who do you think that would have been?"

Shrugging, Lenz looked at the picture. "Kieran, maybe? Or maybe not, since they'd gotten into a fight. Maybe her cousin, David? They sometimes hung out. But it could have been a lot of people — I didn't know most of Ashley's friends from school."

Jake nodded and held up a plastic bag holding a sheet of paper. "I'll see if we can do anything with this, but I'm guessing the blackmailer was smart enough to wear gloves." He handed the bag over to Penelope.

Angling the bag so she could avoid the reflection, Penelope saw a pixelated black-and-white photo printed above text. The picture showed two men sitting at a table laughing, a half-full bottle of bourbon next to two white lines of powder. Lenz was somewhat recognizable from the cowlick. Mathew Scarlet was more of a stretch, but presumably the original picture was of higher quality. The words below read, *Be ready with $10,000 in $100 bills in a brown paper bag tonight at 10pm in the park or you become the headline story tomorrow.*

Penelope handed the note back to Jake. He put it to the side of the desk. "Do you have the money?"

"You think I should pay?"

"I think making a payment will buy us time to investigate. And maybe we'll get lucky and catch them coming back to pick up the money." Jake studied his notes again. "There's not a lot to go on here. If Ashley's story about losing the phone was true, it could be anyone. And if it's not true, we're going to have to dig into the last decade of her life to find out who she might have sent the photos to. Either way, the odds aren't great. You should consider taking this to the police. They have more resources for this sort of thing."

Lenz shook his head decisively. "No. I know how things leak. And too many cops wouldn't mind seeing me knocked down."

Jake leaned back in his chair, no surprise showing on his face. "We'll do what we can, but there are no guarantees. Get the money ready. In the meantime, I'll talk to Detective Sanchez to see if I can get a copy of Ashley's phone records." Jake looked at Penelope. "Anything to add?"

"Just one thing." Penelope regarded Lenz, wishing he wasn't so accustomed to hiding his expressions. "If you hadn't talked to Ashley in person since she left, why were you outside her house the night she was killed?"

CHAPTER 10

*J*ake's gaze stayed neutral, but he raised a hand to rub his mouth, a sure sign he was hiding a smile. By raising his eyebrows, he invited Lenz to answer the question.

Lenz opened his eyes wider. "Who said I was outside her house the night she was killed? I spent yesterday evening taping a segment about Bobby's Bakery that's going to run this Sunday."

Sitting back in her chair, Penelope crossed her arms. "Must be a really short segment. The bakery is closed after lunch on Fridays." Bobby and his wife celebrated Shabbat every week.

"That's..." He trailed off.

"You were seen." Penelope didn't add any specifics. If he didn't know who had seen him, he'd have a harder time crafting a lie.

Lenz blew out a breath. "That's the problem with being on camera. I can't go anywhere without someone noticing." He closed his eyes and shook his head. "Yes, I was there. Ashley and I were supposed to meet up earlier that day. I thought I'd be able to tell if she was lying about the pictures if I saw her in person, but I had an interview that ran long and then she had to go to some wedding rehearsal or something. We agreed to meet afterward at the house she was renting. Then I got stuck on a call with my producer, so I was late."

"What happened?"

"Nothing happened. I got there and knocked on her door, but nobody answered. My call went to voicemail. I figured she got tired of waiting and left." He shrugged one shoulder. "Ashley expected people to wait for her, not the other way around. Or, at least, that's how she was when I knew her. So I left."

"You didn't go into the house?"

"No. My cameraman can back me up. He might have spent the whole time playing games on his phone, but he can verify I wasn't gone from the van long enough to have murdered her."

"Did you see anyone?"

Looking thoughtful, Lenz stared at the ceiling. "There were a few people at the coffee shop where I parked, one couple with a dog in a stroller, and another group of four old women. When I was walking back to the van, I saw another guy, white with short brown hair and one of those beards — what do you call it? A Van Dyke?" He drew a mustache and goatee on his face. "He was maybe in his mid-forties."

Penelope grimaced. Todd didn't deserve to look ten years younger than he really was. "Anyone else?"

"Yeah, some red-head was having a meltdown in her mom-mobile. I tapped on her window to make sure she was okay — you never know when you might get a tip about a good story. She almost drove over my foot." He didn't seem bothered by that. "The old women were still at the coffee shop when I left."

Everything he'd told her fit with what she'd heard from

other people. Penelope sighed. At least she wouldn't have to turn in one of Jake's clients in order to protect her son.

Jake promised to call when he was ready to get set up for the blackmail drop in the park and then escorted Lenz to the front door. Penelope stayed behind so the dogs didn't seize the opportunity to bolt.

Brutus rarely made a break for freedom — he knew where his treats were in the kitchen. But Frodo was an unknown. Penelope leaned down to scratch the little dog's chest. "You'd better work on being extra cute around Jake, buddy. It might take a while to figure out where you're going to go."

"It might take a while for what?" Jake had come in behind her unnoticed.

"Oh, nothing." She stood up. "Mid-forties, my ass. What kind of reporter can't tell when a man is in his fifties?"

"I take it the guy he described walking toward the house fits Todd's description?"

"How many men over the age of twenty-five are trying to pull off a Van Dyke? It's ridiculous." She leaned against Jake's chest. Then she sniffed. "Why do you smell like a skunk?"

"I think that's you."

Penelope sniffed her arm. "I think you're right."

"Sorry, what was that?" Jake put a finger in one ear and wiggled it. "I don't think I heard you."

"Funny guy." They drifted into the kitchen while Penelope recounted her meeting with Hannah. "Lenz did corroborate everyone else's alibis, though, right? He knocked on the door and Ashley didn't answer, so she was presumably already dead. Then Todd comes up with his stupid goatee and goes inside. Meanwhile, poor Hannah is out in the minivan. Lenz sees her drive away, which matches Seth's story. It all fits together."

"It all fits, but it doesn't prove anything." Jake opened the refrigerator, picked up the bag of baby carrots, then put it back down and took the olives and spray cheese instead. He held up the metal can uncertainly. "This is the people cheese, right?"

"The dogs get the same stuff, but yes, that can should be dog slobber free. Unless you already let Brutus lick it." Penelope took it from him and stood on her toes to get the crackers out of the cupboard. "How does it not prove anything?"

"Well, we know everyone was where they said they were *after* Ashley was murdered. But what about fifteen minutes before that? Any one of them could have gone in earlier, killed her, and left."

Penelope thought about that as she made a tower of cheese on the cracker. Then she broke it in half and gave each dog a piece. "That's all you get. Go lie down." She sat at the table. "You have a very devious mind. Yeah, I guess none of them are off the hook. It could have been any of them. Other than Seth, of course, because I would know if he murdered someone."

"If it helps, I don't see Seth having done it either." Jake dug an olive from the jar. "It might not have been any of them."

"We need to talk to Kieran. Though we probably can't today since he's the best man. And David, too, but he's the groom, so he's definitely busy."

Jake narrowed his eyes at her. "*We* need to let Brianna investigate the murder without *our* interference."

"I meant about the blackmail pictures," Penelope lied.

"Of course you did."

Penelope thought about it as she added cheese to another cracker. "Is Ashley in any of those pictures? I wonder if *she* got any blackmail demands. Would she have cared if the pictures were made public? I mean, it would probably make the book sell better. And it's not like there would be any evidence about what really happened that night after all this time, anyway."

Jake gave a pointed look at the can of spray cheese. "If you promise to save me some, I'll see if I can get any information out of Brianna when I talk to her."

CHAPTER 11

*W*hen Jake made the call to Detective Sanchez, Penelope moved into the living room. If she stayed in earshot, she would have to force herself not to interrupt. Jake would have a better chance of getting information if Brianna could forget Jake was no longer her boss.

With a free hour in her pet sitting schedule, she rescued her library book from where she'd left it next to the washer and settled in on the couch to find out what all the fuss was about. Brutus took the other cushion, while Frodo took the higher position on the arm of the couch.

Seth came back to get ready for the wedding a few minutes later.

When the dogs had quieted down enough to talk, Penelope put down *One Wild Night*. "How was golf?"

"Not bad." He grinned. "David was a disaster out there — wedding nerves. Even Kieran's playing couldn't save that pair. Emma's dad was my partner. We won fifty bucks."

"Henry might need it for a divorce lawyer after Joann finds out he was the one who suggested all the changes in the wedding."

"Maybe. Since when do you sit around reading in the middle of the day?" Seth squinted to read the cover of the book. "Oh. That explains it."

"Have you read it?"

He made a face. "Not really my thing." Wandering into the kitchen, he called back, "Do you mind if I make a snack? The reception doesn't start until eight." Both dogs followed him.

"You'll be lucky if Joann doesn't cancel it and throw all the food in the garbage. You can have anything you find." She listened to him rummage in the refrigerator as she read. "The baked cubes of meat on the third shelf are dog food for one of my clients." A container slid back onto the shelf. "Though it might taste okay."

A moment later, a grunt was followed by a thud as something wrapped in foil hit the floor. Penelope grinned. She'd heard that noise more than once. "Don't let the dogs trip you!"

"Thanks for the tip." A few minutes later, he came back with a peanut butter and jelly sandwich on a plate, again followed by both dogs. "So, this is a weird question and I'm probably going to be sorry I asked, but why is there a polaroid of my lit professor on the refrigerator?"

Penelope looked up. "Naked?"

A pained look crossed his face. "I was trying to forget that part. She was old enough to be talking about retiring when I took her fairytale class ten years ago."

"Do you remember her name?"

Seth sank down on the other side of the couch. "Professor Miller? Mueller? Something like that."

"First name Roberta?"

Seth gave her a wry smile. "My professors never had first names."

"Right. Hopefully, we can find some trace of her on the

63

college's webpage. Jake's been trying to identify her for a while."

"Now I feel better about dropping that steak on the floor."

Brutus burped.

Penelope shook her head. "I'll take it out of your allowance."

That got a laugh out of him. Seth shoved the last of the sandwich in his mouth and let Brutus lick his fingers. "I have to go get ready. I'll tell you all the stories in the morning."

Thirty seconds after Seth rushed out the door, Jake came out of his office. Penelope had read the chapter where the politician closed a deal and went out to celebrate. She suspected real political wrangling involved more paperwork, but that might be too boring to use in a novel. Putting the book aside, she raised her eyebrows. "Learn anything interesting?"

"Purcell has decided you aren't a strong suspect."

"Well, I know *I* didn't do it. What else?"

"As far as alibis go, the groom's is terrible, but the best man's is solid." While David had been playing a video game alone in his hotel room, Kieran had been on a video conference call. And because his boss, the assemblyman, had campaigned on a promise of greater transparency, the call had been recorded and published on the politician's website. "I skimmed the video. Kieran is on camera for the entire hour. He couldn't have been killing Ashley at the same time."

Penelope sighed. "Todd had better hope we catch the blackmailer tonight. That might be the only thing that keeps him out of prison."

CHAPTER 12

*A*t nearly ten o'clock, most of the illumination and noise in the park came from the wedding reception at the golf course on the other side of the fence. Penelope matched her walk to a song that had come out before the bride and groom had even been born. Though the park was technically closed after dusk, in reality there were knots of people scattered across the area. Three teenagers sat on the swings talking in low voices. Across the grass, a man and his two small daughters were looking at the night sky through a telescope. Jake was hiding in the trees, invisible in the shadows.

With fifteen minutes to go before the 10 p.m. deadline, Lenz fidgeted on the bench.

Penelope walked both dogs around the perimeter, letting them sniff to their heart's content. Brutus had a tendency to pull her into the trees toward Jake every time they went by, but she didn't think anyone would notice.

"Nothing," she whispered as she walked by Jake for the fifth time. "How much do you think everyone at the wedding reception has had to drink? Would they notice if I went by and took a plate of food?" The corner of the park abutted the parking lot of the golf course clubhouse, where Emma and David's reception was being held.

The trees rustled gently. "Now you know the most important part of any stakeout."

"What's that?"

"Snacks." Plastic crinkled. Brutus sniffed at the smell of beef jerky, while Frodo lifted his leg in the vicinity of Jake's shoe.

"You couldn't have mentioned that before?"

"Check your inside pocket."

Penelope patted the sides of her coat. Unzipping the front, she found the interior pocket and a limp chocolate bar, warm from the heat of her body. "You really are the man of my dreams. Just so you know, I couldn't find the ebook version of those E. E. Cummings poems, but I have a bid pending online for the paperback version."

His quiet laugh floated out from the trees. "Go away and let me concentrate."

Penelope urged the dogs along the path as she ate a square of chocolate. Jake had set up tiny motion-activated cameras at all the park entrances, so even if they missed the blackmailer retrieving the cash, they would still have recordings to look through later.

The teens remained huddled together on the swings, laughing about something. Penelope could see Lenz seated on the bench from almost every part of the sidewalk. When someone approached him, she would have a good view. Jake had made her promise not to get close, reminding her this could be the person who had strangled Ashley. But not many people would assault a woman walking next to a mastiff. In reality, Frodo was far more likely than Brutus to bite someone, but sometimes perception was more important.

Brutus was the first one to notice the high-pitched whine

of the mini drone. He raised his head, trotting forward as he tracked it across the night sky.

Penelope groaned. The mastiff was obsessed with the little flying machines. Somebody — they'd never figured out who — had annoyed the neighborhood by flying a drone with a camera over backyards, recording views through windows, and annoying dogs by buzzing them.

After three days of this, Penelope stopped calling Brutus inside when the drone was flying. Instead, she put him in a down-stay in the backyard and waited next to him. When the mini drone flew down, she tossed bird netting over it. Brutus had been caught in the net as well — by the time Penelope had extracted him, the drone was in tiny pieces of slobbery plastic. Nobody had ever shown up to claim the remains, and that was the end of the problem.

Having destroyed the first one, the mastiff considered it his mission in life to destroy all the rest. Usually that wasn't a problem because most operators flew them too high for even an optimistic mastiff to reach. But this one was flying lower, and as far as Penelope knew, it wasn't illegal to fly them in the park. She didn't want to pay to replace an expensive toy if it flew too close to Brutus.

As she watched, the mini drone flew straight to Lenz and hovered in front of him. He peered at a piece of paper dangling below. Then he reached forward and attached the paper bag with the money to the underside of the drone. The machine rose in the air and flew off to the north.

Penelope stomped the pavement with one pink and orange running shoe. "Dang it!"

So much for getting information on the blackmailer.

Brutus still faced the direction where the drone had disappeared. He was trained — more or less — for scent tracking, not following something flying. But he considered mini drones prey to be destroyed, and he had better hearing than most people.

Penelope scooped up Frodo and started running in the direction Brutus had been pulling. "Let's go get it!"

Brutus galloped forward. Normally, running with Brutus was a recipe for disaster — he thought nothing of dashing in front of his jogging companion so he could sniff something on the other side of the trail, and he was large enough that running into him usually ended up with Penelope on the ground. But tonight he was out in front, lumbering down the sidewalk as fast as he could go.

Penelope's phone rang. She juggled the chihuahua so she could reach into her pocket and answer it. "I'm not approaching! We're just following the drone."

Jake didn't bother arguing about the matter. "Where are you now?"

"Highland and..." She looked around at the houses. Working part time delivering mail meant she was never lost. "Cooper."

"I'll be right there."

Penelope shoved her phone back in her pocket. "Good," she said to Frodo as he bounced in her arms. "You can ride in the car." Even in the dim light, she could see the whites of his eyes.

The drone abruptly changed direction, heading perpendicular to the street. Penelope dug in her heels to keep Brutus from charging across the front lawn of the nearest house. He was fully capable of flattening fences if he wanted something on the other side. Especially if the fences had been erected by the local fence builders. Red and Sons provided value commensurate with the money paid, and they were dirt cheap.

This could be the house. Except all the mail she'd delivered here had been for a retired couple who enjoyed planning holiday cruises they never took. They seemed unlikely candidates for blackmailing Lenz with photos found on a phone lost in New York.

Ignoring Brutus's panting, Penelope listened for the drone. No, the Poniatowskis weren't the blackmailers. The mini drone flew over the house behind them and kept going.

Jake pulled to the curb behind her. "No luck?"

She shook her head and opened the hatchback to load Brutus and Frodo inside. "It changed direction and went over the houses." Each dog got a treat before she closed the hatch and walked around to get in on the passenger side.

"Smart. Keeps them from being followed back home."

Penelope collapsed into the seat to catch her breath. She jogged nearly every day, but she didn't often sprint like that. "What kind of range do those things have on them?"

"A couple miles, usually."

"So we didn't actually learn anything useful."

"Maybe, maybe not." Jake accelerated away from the curb, heading for home. "I got a pretty good look at that drone. Those things aren't cheap. And a lot of people who have them belong to drone racing clubs. I'll get a list of members to see if there are any familiar names."

Penelope's phone rang. Seth. "Hi, honey. How's the reception going?"

His laughter had an edge of hysteria she could hear even over the music and talking. "It's been a memorable day. Hey, I've been told I have to bring some of the leftover food home with me. Do you have any requests?"

In the background, Penelope heard a woman yell. "Are you calling your mom? Tell her she's invited!"

Seth dutifully repeated, "Emma says you're invited."

Penelope looked at her phone, then put it on speaker. "What's going on over there?"

"Joann walked out halfway through the ceremony. While I

was reciting the poem, in fact." Someone near him laughed loudly. "She sent out a message saying the reception was canceled. But Henry's the one who has been paying the bills, and he sent out a message saying it was still on. Most of the people who don't know Emma and David didn't come. So there's a lot of extra food and wine. And champagne." He laughed. "Henry was outside earlier learning to fly a drone. They do drone races here at night. Did you know that? This might be the most fun I've ever had at a wedding reception."

Penelope and Jake looked at each other. He turned the corner toward the golf club and murmured, "I'll call Lenz and tell him we'll talk to him later."

Penelope leaned toward her phone. "You're not driving home from there, are you?"

Seth laughed. "Nope. The wedding planner arranged for drivers at the end of the night. Don't worry."

"We'll be there in a few minutes."

CHAPTER 13

*T*he atmosphere in the golf club banquet hall comprised equal parts disbelief and glee; nobody seemed quite sure what would happen later, but they were determined to enjoy the night. On the dance floor taking up one side of the hall, Emma and David swayed, surrounded by friends bouncing in time to the quick tempo song. One couple practiced swing dancing. Another waltzed a box step. Both guests and catering staff wandered in and out the side doors leading to the golf course.

Henry, the father of the bride, sat at a table near the open door, playing cards with a group of men of the same age. His tuxedo jacket lay draped over his chair. From the pile in front of each man, honey roasted almonds seemed to be the currency.

Seth came in from outside, saw Penelope and Jake, and waved. He swiped two glasses of champagne from a passing tray and handed one to each of them. "I taped the best parts of the ceremony on my phone," he confided as he hugged his mother. Penelope accepted Jake's discreet assistance in staying upright. Then Seth hugged Jake. "Do you want to come learn how to fly a drone? Henry put down a deposit to cover it if any of them are damaged, and he said not to worry about it. Or we could go golfing. It's a little harder in the dark."

Penelope patted him on the shoulder. "You can show us the drones, but we need to congratulate the bride and groom first. And we can't stay long — the dogs are in the car."

"You should have brought them in! Emma wouldn't have minded."

From the way the newlyweds were leaning on each other as they danced, Penelope suspected Emma was at the state of not minding anything at all. "I don't think the caterers are ready to deal with Brutus."

"Right. Right." Seth made a vague gesture toward the door. "I'll get the drones set up."

Watching him walk away, Penelope laughed. "I hope he wasn't planning on doing anything tomorrow morning."

Jake put an arm around her waist as they walked toward the dance floor. "I think we can safely cross Seth off the list of people who might have piloted the drone that picked up the money."

Torn between wanting to defend Seth's skill even while drunk and knowing he wouldn't blackmail anyone in the first place, Penelope shook her head. "He wasn't on my list at all, but I agree."

Dodging the waltzing couple, Penelope tapped on Emma's shoulder. "Congratulations, you two!"

The bride opened her eyes and stood up straight. "Penelope! I'm so glad you made it!"

Penelope found herself in another hug that required assistance from Jake to keep her from staggering backward. "You look lovely." And Emma did, in a strapless mermaid dress with beaded hearts sewn on the bodice.

Emma released her and stood up. "Thank you." She transferred the hug to Jake. "I'm so glad to finally meet you. You're way better than Todd, even if he is my cousin."

Jake's lips quirked at this greeting. "Thank you. Congratulations." He reached past the bride, extending the hand not holding a champagne glass to David. "Hi, I'm Jake, Penelope's husband."

"Nice to meet you." David seemed slightly more sober than his new wife. "Sorry about the invitation mix-up."

Emma raised her head from Jake's chest. "That was my mother. You were both on *my* guest list, but then she took over and every time I tried to say anything, it was all 'let your mother have this one last thing before I die.'" She shook her head, a move that put her so off balance it took both Jake and David to keep her from falling. "It was supposed to be a *short* ceremony."

She said the last two words with great care, then mouthed them again silently. "But then Ashley got famous, so *all* the relatives had to play a role in the ceremony so my mother would have an excuse to invite her. Even though none of us have talked to Ashley for *ten years*." She frowned. "Poor Ashley. Didn't get to read her letter after all." Then she smiled and put a hand on Penelope's shoulder. "But Seth's poem was *lovely*."

"I'm glad it all worked out."

Emma nodded and looked over at the table where her father played poker. "It *did*. We're happy, and my dad's having a good time. There's golfing. And the drones... I think that was my dad. The drones are fun, too."

"Congratulations, again." Penelope helped transfer Emma back to David. "We wish you all the best in the future."

"Thank you." Emma leaned her head against David's shoulder and closed her eyes. They began swaying to a rhythm much slower than the song played by the DJ.

Penelope and Jake slipped away, this time dodging the

swing dancers. "Care to dance?" Jake murmured in her ear as they reached the edge of the floor.

"Yes. But not enough to risk Brutus eating through the seat to get to the front of the car." She kissed his cheek and slid her hand into his. "Let's make a quick stop to say hello to Henry."

Three of the players had folded, leaving Henry and another man Penelope didn't recognize to stare at their cards. As Penelope and Jake arrived at the table, the other man tossed his cards down. "You've had all the luck all evening." The table roared with laughter. Penelope caught a glimpse of Henry's cards before he added them to the deck to be shuffled. He'd been raising with a pair of threes.

Penelope leaned over and put a hand on Henry's shoulder to get his attention. "Sorry to interrupt. We just wanted to add our congratulations on your daughter's marriage. They look like they're very happy together."

Henry pushed his chair back and stood up. "Penelope! Sorry about... well, Joann." He finished his glass of wine. "Never mind. I'm done apologizing for her. I'm glad you came. Go get something to eat!" He held out his hand. "You must be Jake. It's nice to finally meet you."

"Likewise." They shook.

Penelope glanced at the table. "I promised to let Seth show me how to pilot a drone, so we'll let you get back to your game. It was good to see you again."

"You, too." He sat back down. "Who's dealing this round?"

The cool air outside was a quiet relief from the noise inside. Penelope grabbed a skewer with chicken and onions as they walked. "This is why Brutus can't come to wedding receptions. He'd need surgery in less than twenty minutes."

"Yes, *that's* the reason. Nothing to do with slobber, mud, and clothes worth thousands of dollars." Jake reversed suddenly to grab a second prosciutto-wrapped bundle from a tray. "Try this."

Goat cheese filled her mouth, along with something sweet. "Is that persimmon?"

"I don't know, but if we play our cards right, it could be tomorrow's dinner."

"If any of this stuff freezes, we could be done cooking for the rest of the month." She looked over at him. "Would it be tacky to load up before we leave? I mean, we aren't actually on the guest list."

"Technically, we were invited to help eat the food. Not to question people about drones." Jake slanted a glance her way. "Or where everyone was yesterday evening."

"It's lucky we're so good at multitasking, isn't it?"

Music floated through the open doors behind them, but now the buzzing of mini drones could be heard, along with laughter and talking. Penelope and Jake followed the lighted path to a small building fifty feet away with an open hatch similar to a concession stand. An employee in a golf club polo shirt waited inside. On the patio, a knot of wedding guests stood holding controllers. They seemed to be racing along a route that covered most of the golf course. A quiet beep sounded from the controllers when a milestone was passed.

Seth came over, looking at the screen on his controller even as he walked. "You ready to take over, Mom?"

"Absolutely." Window-spying drone aside, she'd always wanted to fly one of these things. And this way, she'd have a better idea of how hard it would be to fly the drone to pick up the blackmail money. "What do I need to do?"

Her son handed her the controller, then pointed to the stick on the right. "Roll and pitch." Then he pointed to the stick on the left. "Yaw and throttle."

Penelope stared at the controller in her hands, then

looked up and frowned at him. "Now explain it for someone who didn't spend their teens playing flight simulators."

He laughed. "This one is faster, slower, left, right, and the other is up, down, and spin around. Try it and you'll see. If you want to join the race, they're going around the course in the same order as the holes are numbered." He looked at Jake. "Let me grab one for you."

Penelope watched the screen, which showed a green-tinted view of a fairway, and started moving the sticks around semi-randomly. The ground grew nearer, then farther away. Another drone zipped by under hers. She meandered around, seeing more golf course under her. "How do I know where I am?"

Seth had returned with another controller for Jake. "Yeah, it's sometimes a little tricky to find a sign you can read from the top." He reached over and hit the button with an icon of a house on the bottom. "But if you really get lost, there's always this option." On the display, the drone gained altitude and began flying across the course with no input from Penelope. He pointed to an open area with three other drones on the ground. "It will land over there without you having to do anything else."

On the screen, the golf course whizzed by. After a minute, the small building came into view, and a moment later, a mini drone landed next to the other three. "For some reason, I thought this would be harder."

Next to her, Jake frowned in concentration as he meticulously worked his way through all the controls. "Right." He zipped down to a sign and maneuvered the drone so it rolled to the side. *9, Par 4*. With a faraway look in his eye, Jake rotated to the left. "And the sand trap should be over... here."

Penelope watched as his drone flew over an irregular sand pit. "No fair. You've been here often enough to know the course layout."

"And you said golf was a waste of time."

Penelope pushed the controller sticks around until her drone rose in the air. She was still experimenting when a caterer walking by with crab cakes distracted her. The panicked yells of a group of partiers brought her back to her task, and she reversed direction before she hit anyone. Shoving the controller at Seth, she said, "Here. You can play for me. I'm going to get something to eat." One look at Jake told her he would be occupied for at least the next fifteen minutes as he learned the intricacies of the controls. "Did your father and Hannah come to the reception?"

Seth nodded without looking up from what he was doing. "They left... I don't know, maybe fifteen minutes ago? Charlotte was kind of cranky and Hannah wanted to put her to bed."

The caterer kindly waited for Penelope to take the last three crab cakes from the tray and promised to return with mini quiches. After he left, Penelope wandered from group to group, watching as they raced the drones against each other. Kieran, the best man and one of Ashley's childhood friends, was easy enough to find; he was the only man in a tuxedo Penelope didn't recognize. He had the perfect face for a politician — attractive without looking like he tried too hard. His brown hair was clipped short on the sides, just long enough for the premature gray at his temples to show.

Next to him, an older man in an expensive suit laughed as he frantically toggled the controls. As she watched, two drones came careening toward the home area. The one in front suddenly dropped, forcing the other drone to the ground. Then the one on top zoomed forward and the older man's controller beeped as it reached the finish line. "Ha! I finally got you, you bastard!" He checked his watch. "I need to say my goodbyes and get some sleep, or I'll have bags under my eyes on *Meet the Press*."

Kieran held out his hand to shake. "We'll have to have a rematch soon."

"Count on it. Contact my office on Monday about that other thing. I'm sure we can set something up." He put the controller down on the shelf of the concession booth and walked back into the building.

Penelope waited until the older man was out of earshot. "Does he know you let him win?"

CHAPTER 14

Kieran turned and raised his eyebrows in surprise, as if he hadn't known she was there. Or at least wanted her to believe that. "The congressman? I assume he knows, but it's expected." He cocked his head. "Have we met? You look familiar."

Penelope took a mini quiche from the passing tray. "Penelope Standing. I was the town's mayor for the blink of an eye." The time between the special election after the previous mayor had fled the country and the next regular election had been just long enough for the developers to realize they didn't want Penelope anywhere near the mayor's office. They had chosen her opponent and financed him well.

"Kieran Engle."

"Nice to meet you. Your kindergarten teacher was just telling me stories about you."

His grin this time seemed less rehearsed. "Really? I should hire you for opposition research during the next campaign."

"We were talking about Ashley."

His face fell. "Ah."

"Sorry for your loss."

Kieran shook his head slowly. The gesture seemed rehearsed, but of course it would be — people must have been offering him condolences all day long. "I still can't believe it. Before last month, we hadn't spoken in over ten years. And now she's gone. We had planned to catch up before dinner, but the rehearsal ran long and I had to go back to my hotel room for a meeting." He cocked his head. "It's the first time I've ever been grateful for our Friday night staff meetings. I almost gave up on the hotel wifi, but I'm glad I didn't. The police have been asking where everyone was when Ashley died. I could prove I was in the hotel."

"That's handy, but why would anyone think it was you? If you really hadn't seen each other since high school..."

"We texted about meeting up, so they came by to interview me." He shrugged. "Ashley always had forty-seven things going on at the same time, so who knows what she was really doing. Some old guy trying to look like he's still in his twenties was hitting on her at the rehearsal. They looked like they were getting cozy." A tiny laugh escaped him. "I'm surprised the cops haven't arrested him yet."

At least some people could see through Todd's ridiculous facial hair, though Penelope wasn't so sure she was happy about the "old" label. She and her ex-husband were the same age. "I'm sure he deserves whatever's coming his way."

Kieran picked up the mini drone controller. "Care for a match?"

"I don't know if everyone is wearing enough protective equipment." At Kieran's confused look, she shrugged. "Sure, why not?"

By the time she had maneuvered the drone to the starting line of the first hole, Penelope could tell Kieran was regretting his offer.

"No, that's the... Okay, I guess that's one way to do it," he said as he watched her using the controller. "Should we just do the first three holes?"

"Sounds good." Penelope didn't mind being terrible at things, but the condescension in his voice made her want to win. "How do we know when to start?"

"Say when."

If she couldn't win through flying skill, maybe she could distract him. "Did you read *One Wild Night*? How close to the truth do you think it got? Oh, and start." She pushed the stick all the way to the side. Instead of rising, the drone spun around. A glance at Kieran's screen showed the green rushing by under his drone. When her drone was finally facing the right direction again, she tried the other stick. The machine leapt forward, skimming just barely over the ground.

"Pure fiction." Kieran glanced at her screen, compressed his lips to hide a grin, and relaxed his shoulders. "You might want to go up a little higher before you run into the hill."

Adding elevation made it easier to scan a larger area. She didn't see Kieran's drone anywhere. Sneaking a glance at his screen, she saw he was hovering above her drone. When she moved forward, he shadowed her. "It wasn't all fiction, though, was it? Mathew Scarlet died at the hotel, and someone in the bar said he picked up a woman and a man that evening." That last bit was a complete fabrication, but she couldn't very well say that Lenz Russell had told her what happened.

"Really? I never heard about that."

"After the book came out, everyone assumed Ashley was the woman. I thought the other person might have been you. Weren't you and Ashley an item back in the day?" She peered at an illuminated hoop suspended in the air. "Is that ring the finish line?"

"Yep. First one through wins the hole." He nudged one

stick to keep his drone aligned over Penelope's. "If there really were other people in the room that night, I wasn't one of them. Ashley and I had drifted apart by our senior year. We were at different schools, so our schedules were different."

"Oh, right, you went to St. Luke's, didn't you?" Getting in a position to go through the hoop took some concentration. She overshot the elevation, then made a series of semi-random maneuvers to get in front of the ring. Finally. She moved forward.

The ground rushed up at her.

A look at Kieran's screen told her the reason. He'd landed on top of her. Then he was up and through the ring in one fluid movement. His controller chimed. "My point."

Penelope gritted her teeth and steered the drone toward the next tee area. It was one thing to be patronizing and let her win. But to be patronizing and then knock her away at the last moment seemed unnecessarily rude. "St. Luke's must have been quite a change after going to a public middle school."

The all-boys Catholic high school was famous for its strict behavior code and antiquated academic guidelines. Nearly any infraction could lead to detention and extra homework; Penelope had heard of one student who'd written twenty essays on the importance of not swearing before he'd finally graduated. He'd celebrated his release a bit too early, and the social media post with a picture of the school and a series of four-letter words had led to his diploma being withheld.

"That's an understatement. But it made me the man I am today." He gestured with his controller. "Say when."

"Now." She was getting the hang of the controller now and sped across the green. Unfortunately, she didn't know where the hole was, and had to stop to look at the course map displayed on the concession stand. By the time she'd figured it out, Kieran's drone was once again hovering over hers. She grimaced. If this was the type of man St. Luke's had made him, his parents deserved a refund. "And you never saw Ashley after she moved to New York? Seems like it would be useful to have a place to stay when visiting."

"New York has excellent hotels."

He was obviously planning to perform the exact same stunt on the second hole. Penelope considered her options. She could try to make it through the ring before he could drop his elevation; that would be ideal, but she doubted her ability to fly in the right direction on the first try. She could try to get out of the way until he went under her and then go through. Or she could give up on the ring altogether and try to knock his drone out of the sky. That last option sounded the most fun.

She lined up her drone near the ring, keeping an eye on Kieran's controller. "It's probably good that Ashley only wrote fiction. People aren't too forgiving about anything in a politician's past, even things that happened during high school."

Kieran pulled the left stick all the way down. Penelope banked her drone to the right, then moved forward. She clipped the side of the ring, making it through right before Kieran went through the center. Her controller chimed.

"Nice move, Mrs. Standing."

"It's Ms. Standing. I've never been a huge fan of women being forced to change their names after marriage."

"Not big on tradition? Have to be careful about that if you get into politics."

Penelope flew the drone toward the start of the third hole. "Everyone in town already knows all about me. And it's not like I would ever run for office at the national level." Both drones hovered above the tee area. "Ready?"

"Go."

This time Penelope had been smart enough to look at the course map ahead of time. Avoiding the dogleg on the green, she went straight up, over the trees, then back down toward the ring glowing in the darkness. A glance at Kieran's controller told her he had done the same thing. "But at least I did learn one thing about politics when I was mayor."

"What's that?"

"Everyone seems to respect politicians who cheat. It's weird how people are okay with that." Her drone suddenly skittered to the side. Apparently, Kieran had decided she was enough of a threat now to deserve his attention.

He looked over and grinned. "It's just how the game is played. There really is no cheating when you figure that out."

Penelope shook her head. "And that's why I would never run for national office. But as long as that's how you feel..." She leaned over and pushed the homing button on his controller.

It only took him three seconds to shut down the automatic return, but that was just long enough for Penelope to sail through the ring.

Her controller chimed. "Two out of three. I think that means I win." She tapped the home button and put the controller on the ledge of the concession stand.

Kieran stared at her for a long moment. Then he laughed loudly, the sound competing with the music coming from inside the banquet hall. "I think I like you, Ms. Standing. We'll have to do this again sometime."

Penelope gave a non-committal smile. "Maybe." She looked around. "Did you see where that tray of crab cakes went?"

CHAPTER 15

Settled on the couch later that evening with her back against Jake's shoulder and Brutus weighing down her feet, Penelope waited for Jake to finish his call with Lenz Russell. He finally hung up with a sigh and turned his attention to the cricket match playing on the muted television. Frodo jumped up to the back of the couch and lay down with his front feet on Jake's shoulder, close to Penelope's head. Jake held his breath. Then the dog put his head down on his paws and closed his eyes.

After marking her spot in the book and closing it, Penelope leaned around to scratch Frodo's cheek. "How did Lenz take it?"

"About like you'd expect. He's disappointed, but he knew the possibility of catching the blackmailer tonight was low." Jake slowly turned his head to look at the dog next to his ear. "He's not just getting into a good position to maul me, right?"

"No. He's cuddling." Penelope had seen Frodo in that same position in Ashley's selfies. "Though, if he *was* going to maul something other than your ankles, this would be the way to do it. But he's not that sneaky."

"I'll take your word for it." Jake slowly tilted his head to rest against the chihuahua. Frodo let out a deep sigh.

That was Penelope's cue to return to her regular slouch. "It almost has to be a guest at that wedding."

"Or an employee of the golf club. Or someone who knew there was an event at the club tonight and wanted to confuse the issue."

"But..."

Jake watched the cricket match as they finished an over, then he sighed. "But I think you're right. It was probably a guest at the wedding." He shifted his hand to stroke a strand of hair away from her face and froze when Frodo growled. "Your new boyfriend needs to chill, or he needs to sit somewhere else."

"He's had a rough couple of days. He'll relax."

Jake's voice held a skeptical edge. "If you say so. Did you learn anything while we were there?"

"I learned I should be putting basil in my crab cakes."

Jake slowly moved his head so he could see her more clearly. "You make crab cakes?"

"Once. Before Seth was born. When I was still convinced I needed to learn how to cook so I could attract a man." She paused and lifted her brows. "Did you say something?"

"Do I look that stupid? There's no comment I could make that wouldn't end up with me and Brutus sharing the sofa while the little land shark takes over my half of the bed."

Penelope patted his face. "That's why I married you. Well, that and the way you vacuum."

"I am a pro at vacuuming."

"The best I've ever seen." She looked at the cover of the book as she thought. "Kieran could definitely have flown the drone that picked up the money. But I think most of the people there could have, despite all the alcohol. Even *I* might have been able to manage it if I'd stayed a little longer."

"But how many ambulances would we have needed to call in the meantime?"

Penelope elbowed him lightly. "Very funny. Kieran was pretty quick to tell me he had an alibi. Though I feel like he was kind of shirking his best man duties by pointing out David was off playing video games on his own at the time." She shook her head. "Can you track video game usage? I'll have to ask Seth. One of Brianna's people is probably looking into it, too, I bet."

After a pregnant pause, Jake abandoned the cricket to look at her. "Oh, sorry, that was my cue, wasn't it? I'll ask Brianna tomorrow. She's coming over in the morning to get a statement from Seth."

"Good. And did you learn anything tonight? Other than how to fly a mini drone? And don't think I haven't seen you checking how much it would cost to buy one of those things."

"Purely for the case. Our blackmailer might have purchased one."

"Right."

Jake cleared his throat. "I learned Ashley told a couple of people she was going to read a letter at the ceremony, but nobody knows if it was something she wrote or something someone else wrote to her."

"It was probably on her laptop. I could have looked while I was there, but I would have had to step over her body. That seems a little rude."

Jake snaked an arm around her waist, ignoring Frodo's growls. "And I learned how good you look sprinting across the park."

"Talk like that is going to get you back on Frodo's side of the bed."

He laughed. "It's already Frodo's side?"

"We could go upstairs to discuss it. Unless you want to see who wins the cricket game."

The television went dark as Jake hit the remote. "It's only the first day of the match. They'll play the highlights tomorrow."

* * *

THE MORNING AIR was brisk as Penelope glanced over her shoulder to check for traffic, then jumped off the curb, Heidi keeping pace by her side. The German shepherd did her own check, though she looked for other dogs and squirrels. Not that she would chase after either of them, but she liked to be on the lookout.

Penelope angled their path so they would pass by the Box House. "Not to look for clues," she explained to the dog as they jogged. "But if we don't go by there soon, I'll start thinking of it as the place where people get murdered and avoid it forever."

Heidi flicked an ear in agreement.

Being her own boss meant never having to sit through another performance review. It also meant Penelope could rearrange her schedule so she'd be back home when Brianna or one of the other detectives came by to take Seth's statement. Meanwhile, Jake was taking Frodo and Brutus for their morning walk, hoping the additional time together would convince the chihuahua to stop growling at him. Sooner or later, the police would track down Ashley's mother and then Frodo would be her problem.

Mis-aimed sprinklers had washed the pollen from the sidewalk, but everything else seemed unchanged as they went around the corner and the Art Deco house came into view. She'd half expected to see crime scene tape fluttering near the front door, but it looked just the same as it had two days ago when she'd arrived. Even most of the cars parked on the street were in the same spot, though the white van had been in the coffee shop parking lot. On Friday she hadn't noticed the Channel 8 news logo — this was the van Lenz Russell had been in.

"Probably came back to do a story at the house before they rent it out to the next person," she told Heidi. The dog glanced up, tongue lolling to the side as she trotted along. Would having a famous person murdered in the house be good or bad publicity? Penelope wasn't sure. "I wouldn't stay there," she confided to the dog as they ran toward the house. "But that's only because of that hideous bathroom wallpaper."

There was no movement in the van as Penelope drew closer. She scanned the street, looking for Lenz. Surely he wouldn't have gone *into* the house. Even without tape in front of the door, it had to be considered a crime scene.

A dark red smear broke up her reflection on the van's rear bumper.

Penelope stumbled to a halt. The side of the van didn't have any windows, probably to reduce the theft of expensive equipment. Had she really seen what she'd thought she'd seen on the bumper?

For just a moment, she considered continuing on her run. If there was something wrong, someone else could deal with it. But after more than five decades, she knew herself well enough to understand she'd spend the entire rest of the run wondering. Besides, Lenz could have been hurt, and he was Jake's client. She turned and retraced her footsteps until she was standing behind the van.

That smear definitely looked like dried blood, as if someone had dragged someone injured out of the van. Or perhaps they had dragged roadkill *into* the van for some reason. But while the rest of the van was covered in a gentle dusting of pollen, the blood smear was pollen-free.

The vehicle had two rear doors, and both had windows, but they were darkly tinted and covered in an anti-theft grill.

Penelope grimaced at Heidi. "If I call the police now and they show up and find out it was just a dog with a bloody ear that brushed against the van, I'll never hear the end of it."

Heidi panted, her tail lower than its usual position.

Penelope made a pact with herself. If the door was unlocked, she'd peek inside. If it wasn't, she would call Jake and let him deal with it. Hoping that it was locked, she pressed the button on the handle. The latch clunked under her hand, and the door opened.

The back of the van was filled with cameras and computers and other expensive-looking equipment. There wasn't enough room for a man to lie down, and just enough space for a body to sit wedged against the door.

Which is why the dead man fell backward into Penelope and then slid down to the asphalt.

CHAPTER 16

This time, Penelope got to give her statement directly to Detective Brianna Sanchez. They sat at a table outside the coffee shop while Chief Purcell paced around the van and got in the rest of the team's way.

Brianna looked like she couldn't decide if Penelope was making it up or if the story was so weird it had to be true. "You were just running by."

"Yes."

"And you saw something on the bumper, so you decided to open the van because you thought there might be a body inside."

Penelope grimaced. Put like that, it did sound bad. "If I could have seen through the back windows, I wouldn't have opened the door. But they're tinted."

"The door was unlocked?"

"Unfortunately."

"Okay, so then describe the next part to me, so I'm sure I have it right in my notes."

Penelope took a steadying breath. "I opened the door, and the body must have been pressing against it, because it fell toward me." She made a motion with her hand toward her chest, only then realizing there was a smear of blood on her shirt. "And I kind of jumped back and he fell on the ground."

Brianna nodded solemnly. She appeared to be biting her cheek. "So, where does the dog fit into all this?"

Penelope put a hand out to rub Heidi's chin. "Look at it from Heidi's perspective. The door opened and somebody attacked me. She was just being protective."

"By ripping up the dead guy's arm."

"Just a little." By the time Penelope had gotten over having a dead guy fall on her, Heidi had a good grip on the man's sleeve and was throwing her head from side to side, dragging the corpse with her. Penelope dropped her hand to her lap. "I thought about not saying anything, but then you might think whoever killed him had an attack dog, and..."

Brianna held up one hand. "No. It's good that you told me." She rubbed her face and muttered something that sounded like *Purcell's going to have kittens.* Then she looked at her notebook again. "And you're sure you've never seen this guy before?"

"No. I mean, yes, I've never seen him. I was *expecting* it to be Lenz Russell, but it wasn't."

Brianna nodded slowly. "You were expecting..."

"Lenz Russell. Because he's the Channel 8 reporter and he knew Ashley, so I thought he'd come back to do a story." She remembered what he'd said about the night Ashley was killed. "I think he has a cameraman who travels with him. Maybe that's who that is?" And then it struck her. "Has anyone seen Lenz? He's not dead in the van, too, is he?"

"He is not dead in the van," Brianna replied in carefully even tones.

Penelope glanced at her shirt again. "Do you need me anymore? I need to change and take Heidi home." She couldn't possibly be a suspect — rigor mortis had set in, which meant he'd been dead... two hours? Four hours? Penelope read enough mystery novels that she felt she ought to know that. In any case, he'd been dead for a while, so it couldn't have been her.

Brianna flipped her notebook closed. "Yeah, we're done." She looked over Penelope's shoulder. "Tell Jake to call me when he has a chance."

Penelope turned to see Jake waiting in the car. She waved, and he smiled but didn't get out of the car. Given the way Chief Purcell was still ranting next to the van, Penelope thought that was a wise choice.

A flatbed tow truck arrived, and Brianna stood up. "I have to deal with this. Do me a favor and just... don't find any more bodies for a few days, okay?"

* * *

"YOU WOULD THINK she might be a little more grateful," Penelope complained to Jake and Seth as she came downstairs, freshly showered and in clothes without evidence from a crime scene on them. "The body wasn't getting any easier to examine as it sat in the van."

"I'll be sure to tell her." Jake said, handing her a plate with a grilled cheese sandwich.

"For me?" She peeled back the top layer of bread. "And with jalapeños? You're going all out today." Keeping the plate away from Brutus's nose, she slid into her seat at the kitchen table. Next to her, Seth sat in front of a plate of dry toast holding a glass of water, his messy hair and glazed expression speaking of a long night. Penelope patted his shoulder. "Not quite the same drinking in your thirties as it was in your twenties, is it?"

He groaned. "When did I get so old?"

Penelope and Jake exchanged a smile over Seth's head. She pushed her plate toward her son. "Hungry?"

Seth shuddered. "You used to be a nice person."

"No, I just used to hide my true nature better." She looked at Jake as he fried another grilled cheese, this one without spicy peppers. "Is someone still coming over to talk to Seth today, or has that been put off because of the second body?"

Seth blinked. "The what?"

"There was another murder." Penelope took a big bite and let the zing of the pepper meld with the oozing cheese. "My compliments to the chef."

Seth waved to get her attention. "Who died?"

"I'm not completely sure." Penelope coughed as a pepper seed hit her tongue. "I suspect it was the Channel 8 cameraman, but I'm not sure the police knew his name yet when we left."

With a wince at the motion, Seth turned to look at Jake. "I thought you retired."

Holding up the spatula in defense, Jake shook his head. "Oh, no. You can't blame this one on me. I'm not the one opening up blood-smeared vans."

Penelope snorted into her sandwich. "Well, maybe I wouldn't find so many bodies if other people did their civic duty."

Jake blinked and turned back to the frying pan. "Remind me, does looking for bodies come before or after voting and taking up arms for the common defense in the duties of a good citizen?"

Penelope pointed her sandwich at him. "I'm only letting you get away with that because of the jalapeños." She took another bite. "But you never answered my question. Is Brianna still coming over to talk to Seth today?"

The doorbell rang before Jake could speak. Brutus's barks shook the floor, while Frodo added a high-pitched accompaniment. Seth groaned as he moved to get up, and Penelope patted his arm again. "You stay here and hydrate. I'll let the detective in." And maybe find out if the dead man was who she thought he was.

But when she opened the door, Frodo in one arm and her leg blocking Brutus from moving forward, it wasn't Brianna on the other side. It was Penelope's ex-husband.

CHAPTER 17

"Todd." Seeing him at her house led to multiple questions, but she went with the obvious. "Why are *you* here?"

Safely contained in Penelope's arms, Frodo growled. Brutus tried to push past her to sniff this new person.

Like Seth, her ex-husband looked like he'd had a rough night. His clothes were wrinkled, and the ridiculous Van Dyke beard hadn't been trimmed. The stubble made him look his age. "Your husband is a private investigator now, right?" He glanced toward the street. "Can I come in?"

Penelope gave that question more consideration than she usually did. Then she grabbed Brutus's collar and stepped back. "Sure. Why not?" As soon as Todd had entered, she pushed the door closed and set both dogs free. Brutus immediately pushed Todd against the wall and sniffed him thoroughly while Frodo growled and blocked his escape. Penelope walked back to the kitchen and dropped into her chair at the table. "Jake, you might have another client."

From the living room came a squeaky plea. "Help?"

Seth lifted his head. "Is that Dad?"

Nodding, Penelope raised her voice. "Quit playing with the dogs and come into the kitchen. Jake's busy."

Seth raised one brow and shook his head. Then he picked up his untouched toast and dropped it on the floor.

Brutus barreled into the room, Frodo at his heels. Todd followed hesitantly a few seconds later.

Penelope frowned at her son. "We don't feed the dogs food from the table. It makes them beg every time we sit down to eat."

Her son was unrepentant. "Sorry. It fell." He shifted his attention to his father. "Why are you here?"

Penelope nodded. "That's what *I* said."

After transferring the spatula to his left hand, Jake held out his right. "Hi. I'm Jake. You must be Todd. I've heard a lot about you."

Todd's smile was strained as they shook. "Nice to meet you."

Jake pointed at Brutus, who had gone back to sniff Todd again. "You lie down on your bed." Then he raised a brow at Frodo. "You, too."

Both dogs went to the edge of the kitchen, where Brutus's bed took up the entire corner. Frodo perched in the middle. Brutus took the edge and sprawled onto the tiles.

Jake tossed them each a cheddar crumble and turned back to the pan. "Are you hungry? I can make you a grilled cheese, if you'd like."

"No, thanks." Todd eyed Seth and turned back to Jake. "Is there somewhere we can talk in private?"

"Why don't you go on into the office. I'll be there just as soon as this is done." Jake pointed in the right direction. Todd edged past the dogs and went into the office.

Jake followed and closed the office door, then came back to the stove. "You okay with him as a client?"

Penelope shrugged. "As long as you are."

Seth looked up from his contemplation of the tabletop. "Do I get a vote?"

"No." Penelope softened the answer by pushing his glass closer. "Drink your water. It will make your head feel better."

With a flourish, Jake flipped off the stove. "Maybe I should talk to him alone, at least at first."

Penelope waved him on his way. "Call me if you need to hide the body."

The doorbell rang again, setting off another dog stampede. This time, it was Brianna. Penelope invited her in and sent Brutus off to his bed in the kitchen. "Jake's with a client."

Brianna leaned down to let Frodo sniff her hand. "I'm just here to get Seth's statement."

"The good news is he was way too drunk to kill anyone last night."

Seth came out of the kitchen, his face damp, as if he had just splashed water on it. "Stop talking me into trouble, Mom." He held out a hand and smiled with a touch of the charm his father had once possessed. "Hi, I'm Seth."

"Detective Sanchez." She straightened her shoulders. "Is there someplace you and I can talk?"

Penelope took that to mean Brianna didn't want her butting in. "You two can have the living room. I'll go into the kitchen and finish my lunch." From there, she could listen to Seth and Brianna, and she could get up and eavesdrop on Jake if she wanted.

Brianna narrowed her eyes, as if she'd seen straight through Penelope's strategy, but she caught Seth's eye and nodded toward the sofa. "Shall we?"

Penelope went back to the kitchen table, scrolling through her phone as she listened with half an ear to Seth explaining what he had seen and done on Friday evening. Channel 8 had already posted a tribute clip, which told Penelope the dead man's name was Sam Deu and he'd worked as a cameraman for seventeen years. She also learned Lenz Russell was alive and well — he was the one reading the tribute.

As she chewed her sandwich absently, she thought about that. The two deaths *had* to be connected. The obvious answer was that Sam Deu had seen something, or some*one*, the night Ashley had been killed. Lenz had mentioned there had been a cameraman waiting in the van who could give him an alibi.

Had *Lenz* killed him? Maybe the alibi didn't exist, and the cameraman wouldn't lie for him. But why bring him up in the first place? And since Lenz worked with Sam, he could presumably have met him anywhere. Why murder him at the Box House, where the police couldn't possibly miss the connection?

No, it didn't make sense for Lenz to kill him, at least not in that location. So why had Sam returned to the scene of the crime? Unless the murderer found him there independently, they must have been planning to meet. Had Sam been trying to blackmail the killer? That would suggest he'd also been the one blackmailing Lenz, unless they had two separate black-mailers, which seemed unlikely. Or... Lenz was ambitious, always looking out for the next big story. Maybe Sam was trying to prove his worth by digging up leads on his own.

It all went back to the first murder. Why had Ashley been the target? Was it because of something she had planned to read at the wedding? Or because of whatever it was that had made her flee to New York all those years ago?

Penelope remembered her copy of *One Wild Night*, still sitting on the coffee table in the living room. Maybe she could find something in there.

* * *

JAKE WAS STILL in his office with Todd when Brianna had finished taking Seth's statement and left. Her son wandered into the kitchen, opened the refrigerator door, and in a too-casual voice said, "She seems nice."

Penelope turned the page and reminded herself she had vowed not to meddle in his private life. Luckily, the door to Jake's office opened before she could reply. Todd's shoulders were more relaxed, and he looked at ease with the world. Penelope knew that look. He'd dumped his problems on someone else, and now those problems didn't seem as large. In her experience, that meant he had absolved himself from all wrong-doing and wouldn't learn anything. She sighed and waited for Jake to show him out.

Seth found the container of salmon rolls, popped two in his mouth, then caught sight of the clock on the wall. "Crud, I have to get going. I promised Emma and David I'd help them move the wedding gifts." He chugged the rest of his glass of water and ran to the guest room.

Walking back into the kitchen, Jake turned his head to watch Seth. "Ah, the miraculous healing powers of youth and aspirin."

"Or maybe talking to a pretty woman. What did Satan want?"

"Todd hired me to find out who's trying to get him arrested."

Penelope repurposed a flyer advertising a new restaurant as a bookmark and closed the novel, giving Jake her full attention. "Very bold of him to assume it's not me."

"Or smart. Who better to learn all your secrets?"

"The day you learn all my secrets will be the day I poison your coffee."

Jake's lips twitched. "I think I'm fairly safe."

Penelope smiled back, aiming for coquettish, but giving

up after Jake's smile widened. "So why does he think some-one's trying to get him arrested?"

"Because he got a text from an unknown number last night telling him to go to the Box House early this morning to buy back footage of him entering the house the day Ashley died."

"Another blackmailer?" Then the implication hit her. "Hang on. Did Todd leave *another* body for me to find? That *jerk*!"

Jake cleared his throat. "Apparently, his powers of obser-vation aren't as good as yours. He drove over, waited near the van for thirty minutes, and then left. He never noticed the blood smear on the bumper."

"Not a huge surprise. He never noticed Seth's diaper needed changed either."

Putting one hand on her shoulder, Jake looked into Pene-lope's eyes. "It's been thirty years. You might have to let that one go."

"Never." She pecked him on the cheek. "I'm guessing you told him to tell the police."

Jake's expression turned sour. "He's hoping nobody saw him and it won't be necessary."

That sounded like Todd — pretend there wasn't a problem and hope it went away. The annoying part — to Penelope, anyhow — was that more often than not, his approach worked. Of course, when it didn't, things tended to go spectacularly wrong. "You know I love you and I want your investigation business to succeed, right? But if you happen to fail at this one particular case, I won't hold it against you."

Jake put an arm around her. "Think of Seth."

From the living room, Seth spoke up. "Why do you need to think of me?" He appeared in the doorway, face scrubbed, hair combed, with his keys and wallet in one hand. "Should I be worried?"

Penelope waved a hand at him. "No, Jake's just trying to make me a better person. Have a good time."

"Thanks."

Penelope waited until the front door had closed behind her son. "Fine. I agree — provisionally — it would probably be better if Seth's father didn't go to prison for a murder he didn't commit."

"I'm proud of you."

Now that she'd gotten that out of the way, Penelope allowed herself to focus on the problem. "If someone really was trying to set up Todd for Sam Deu's murder, they must have known Todd was there the night Ashley died."

"Not too surprising. It's likely the same person murdered both people."

"Right, but how would they have known who Todd was?" She looked at the cover of the book, which showed blood dripping down from the top edge to partially obscure a femme fatale figure seen from behind. "The only place Todd and Ashley overlap is the wedding."

"They could have gotten Todd's number from Ashley's phone," Jake pointed out.

Penelope's shoulders slumped. "Ashley's phone. I forgot about that. Todd's texts would have been at the top because he's a slimeball who leaves his pregnant wife at home with a toddler so he can flirt with another woman." She made a face. "I take it back. I'm okay with Todd going to jail."

Jake put his hand over hers. "How about I work on this one on my own?"

"Don't worry. As tempting as it might be, I won't let that jerk get arrested for this. Hannah doesn't need the extra stress." She stood up and kissed the spot where Jake's gray hair merged into the brown. "I need to walk some dogs. Maybe that will shake an idea loose."

CHAPTER 18

*P*enelope had always thought better while in motion, a quirk that had caused many parent-teacher conferences when she was a child. It wasn't that she had *tried* to disturb her classmates with her non-stop movements; it was just that the minute she started concentrating on the subject, she forgot to hold still. Adulthood had many privileges, chief among which was that nobody could tell her to sit quietly in her seat all day long.

"It's a puzzle," she told Ruggles as the English bulldog shuffled next to her on the sidewalk. He sniffed a mailbox pole and lifted his leg. "The blackmailer and the murderer *have* to be the same person." Ruggles moved forward to the rosemary bush six inches away and repeated the process. "Or do they?"

Ruggles was no athlete, even for a bulldog. On their half-hour walks, they often got no farther than three houses away. Once, he'd put on an early burst of speed and they'd gone three blocks, but then Penelope had to carry him back.

"If the killer *isn't* the blackmailer," she continued, as Ruggles carefully examined the patch of grass where he'd once found half a donut, "then the blackmailer just happened to pick the same time to meet my worthless ex-husband as the killer did to meet Sam Deu."

Penelope stopped talking to the dog and nodded to a woman walking by. When the woman was far enough away, Penelope frowned about her previous theory. "No."

Ruggles tilted his head to assess whether he needed to stop snuffling at the grass. From that, Penelope assumed "no" was a word he heard with some regularity. She leaned over to scritch his rear end. "You're fine. I didn't mean you."

She straightened. "I think it's all the same person. But who? Kieran has an alibi. David would have been too busy with all the wedding stuff. Lenz wouldn't blackmail himself. Todd has thousands of faults, but I just can't see it. And Seth and Hannah... I refuse to consider them." She sighed and followed Ruggles to the next bush. "There must have been someone else there."

The bulldog did his usual about-face and ambled toward his home, stopping at the same bushes he'd marked just moments before.

Penelope nodded. "You're right. I need to find out what happened in Ashley's past that was so important someone killed her to keep her quiet."

Ruggles snorted and kept walking.

* * *

No other breakthroughs occurred to Penelope while she was scooping litter boxes and filling food bowls. By the time she headed home, her to-do list consisted of reading Ashley's book and asking Seth who could tell her about Ashley's high school years.

When Brutus and Frodo merely popped their heads out of the kitchen to see who had come in, Penelope deduced something more important was happening there, probably involving food. "I'm home," she called. "If you're feeding the dogs appetizers from the wedding, you're staying downstairs tonight to let them outside."

"Not guilty."

Penelope followed Jake's voice into the kitchen and found a red-haired woman seated at the table. At first glance, Penelope thought the other woman was her own age, but the hands holding a mug of tea bumped up her estimate by at least a decade, possibly two. Her face, though... Those eyes hadn't changed in forty years. "You're Roberta!"

That elicited a warm smile with a hint of ruefulness. "Guilty as charged." Age may have reduced her vocal strength, but her diction remained perfect. It reminded Penelope of the way Esther spoke when talking to a group of people. She supposed teaching involved the same need to vocally project, whether it was to kindergartners or college students.

Glancing over his shoulder as he pulled a tray of miniature quiches from the oven, Jake said, "This is my wife, Penelope Standing. And this is Professor Stacks."

"Not a professor yet when those pictures were taken."

Penelope reflexively glanced at the refrigerator and was relieved to see Jake had taken the photos down. Then she caught sight of one on the table. Now she had to say something. "They're very tastefully done."

Roberta laughed out loud. "Maurice would have been delighted to hear you say that." She sipped her tea and her lips quirked. "Personally, I thought it was just a bit of harmless smut. Things were different back then. I didn't need to worry about them being posted on social media. Grad school was expensive, and it was much easier to spend a few hours posing for Maurice than working weekends in the cafeteria."

Penelope nodded. "I never finished college." She'd gotten

married and pregnant, and then they hadn't had the money for tuition and childcare. "Maybe if I'd met Maurice, I'd have a degree."

Jake cleared his throat, looking slightly alarmed. He set the platter of quiches on the table. "Help yourself. Let me get the paperwork."

The women watched him go. Penelope grinned as she got out plates and forks. "He's afraid I'm going to take up pole dancing if we run out of money."

Roberta chuckled. "Men. What is it you do?"

"Pet sitting. And I sometimes fill in delivering mail."

"Ah, you stay active. That's good."

Penelope waited until she could hear Jake coming back into the kitchen. "Yes, that will be useful if I need to do burlesque dancing to pay the bills."

Jake set a sheet of paper in front of Roberta. "We just need your name, address, and social security number, plus an attestation that you're the one in the photo. They'll mail a check to you when all the claims on the estate are settled." He turned his head to look at Penelope. "Just remember to keep track of your tips so we can file our taxes correctly."

Roberta laughed again, the sound filling the room.

With *One Wild Night* on the table, there wasn't enough space for Roberta to write without having her arm at an awkward angle, so Penelope reached over to pick up the book. Roberta stopped her with a hand on the cover, read the title, then nodded. "Ah. I suppose this will have another round of publicity after the unfortunate event. It's too bad, really. She might have done some good work if she'd lived longer."

Penelope bit into a ham and cheese quiche, ignoring Brutus's raised head and begging gaze. "You've read it?"

"Mm. I used it in class last semester. *Sex and Modern Women Writers.*" She quirked an eyebrow. "Ridiculous course title, I know, but you have to do something to get the students interested. If nobody signs up, the course gets dropped, and the administration uses that as another reason to cut the budget." With a tilt of her head, she added, "I can teach critical thinking to young minds with any text. It doesn't require books from dead white men."

Penelope regarded the stylized blood drips on the cover in front of her. The novel seemed a little... lowbrow for a college class, but Seth had taken a class that analyzed social media posts, so maybe nothing was off-limits. She was afraid a critique from a scholar would ruin her enjoyment of the book, but she still had to ask. "And what did you think of it?"

Roberta's pen stilled. "Overall, it was a powerful indictment of the gender and age gap in politics."

"Ah." Penelope nodded and tried to look as if her analysis wouldn't have been along the lines of *The plot is interesting, and most of the action is entertaining, but the sex scenes are a little boring*.

Roberta grinned and met her eye. "It's highly readable. I have some quibbles about a few chapters — at times, the style changed enough that it felt as if a different person wrote some sections. I don't think it was an intentional shift. At least, if it was, I couldn't see the point of it. But it certainly wasn't a terrible book, and I thought the author had an interesting way of interjecting different viewpoints in a manner one rarely sees in modern literature."

"If I could talk about a book like that, my friend Esther would let me back into her book club." Penelope flipped the book over to look at the full-page author photo. "I've been reading it to figure out why Ashley might have been killed. There are parts that match real events."

Roberta raised her brows. "Are there? It's been long enough that I've forgotten many of the details. I may have to give it another read with that in mind." She scrawled her signature at the bottom of the paper and put her pen back in her purse. "I think that ought to do it."

Jake took the paper from her and placed it in an envelope with the polaroid. "I'll get in touch if the lawyer needs anything else. After everything is settled, they'll return the original picture to you as well, so you won't need to worry about it getting out."

With a shrug, Roberta waved that thought away. "I have tenure. And the students never believe us old people were once young ourselves." She stood. "It's been lovely to meet you both. Thank you for getting in touch."

Penelope walked her to the door while Jake distracted the dogs. "If you reread *One Wild Night* and you think of anything that might be helpful, can you let me know?" She dug one of her pet sitting cards from her pocket and handed it over.

"Of course. And if you decide you want to study literature, the *Sex and Modern Women Writers* lectures are online. You might enjoy going back to school. You can enroll in any class through the university extension and earn credits toward a degree, if that's something you're interested in."

Penelope stopped her automatic reply that she was too old to go back to school. "Thanks. I'll think about it." She closed the door and leaned against it as she thought.

The degree, in itself, wasn't a draw; she hadn't needed it to qualify for part-time mail delivery, and she didn't intend to find a job working for someone else ever again. But it might be nice to have a *goal*, just to give her something to work toward while she kept her brain from turning to mush.

But first she had to find a way to get her ex-husband back out of her life.

CHAPTER 19

*T*he miniature quiches were quickly devoured as they discussed plans for tracking down Lenz Russell's blackmailer, who might also be the killer. Jake stood and picked up the platter. "Shrimp? Or should we just skip straight to the cheesecake?"

Penelope's answer was forestalled by Brutus and Frodo bolting for the front door. A few seconds later, Seth's voice called out, "Is everyone decent?"

"Yes, it's safe to come in." Penelope smiled at her husband and lowered her voice. "I have no idea why he thinks he needs to ask that."

"You *did* walk through the house in your underwear when Lenz came over," Jake pointed out.

"But Seth doesn't know that." Then she sprang to her feet as a high-pitched cry of surprise caught her ear. A small child was at the door with her son. "Hold on a second. I'll grab the dogs."

Since Seth's friends rarely brought children with them, she wasn't surprised to find Hannah and her toddler huddled in the entryway while Seth, the whites of his eyes showing, held his half-sister and fended off Brutus. Hannah's face was red and tear-streaked; her blouse looked like half a toddler's meal had been spilled on it. She had a diaper bag slung over one shoulder and a suitcase in the other hand.

Charlotte began to cry when she saw Jake, leaning toward her mother with both arms out. Penelope changed her tactics. In general, children loved Jake, but some found any unknown man frightening. "You corral the dogs," she told Jake. "I'll..." She waved her hands.

Jake kissed her temple as he passed her. "I owe you," he whispered.

Seth looked faintly apologetic. "Sorry, I should have called when we were still in the car so you could crate the dogs."

"Not a problem." The fact that he hadn't was probably related to his air of panic. "Come on in, everyone. Have a seat on the sofa. Hannah, do you want water to drink, or would tea be better? We have camomile and whatever else comes in that variety pack."

Hannah took a shaky breath as she sank down onto the couch. "I don't need... Water, maybe? Sorry to invade your home. I just wasn't sure where else to go and the police are at the motel and..."

Penelope smiled, pretending she wasn't eager to find out what had happened. "I'll get you some water. Does Charlotte have a sippy cup she likes to use...?"

In the chaos of the next few minutes, Seth found time to sidle over to her in the kitchen and whisper, "Sorry to just show up like this, Mom. The cops searched Dad's motel room and took away something with blood all over it. They arrested him. Dad and Hannah had a reservation for tonight, but the police still have the room and the motel told Hannah the other rooms were fully booked. I didn't think she should drive back home in this state..."

Penelope gave him a quick hug. "You did the right thing. I

may need you to watch Charlotte for a while so we can get everything straightened out."

"Sure. I can do that." He sounded more as if he were trying to convince himself than replying to her. Relations between Seth and his father had been cool for years — Penelope wasn't sure how much time he'd spent around his half-sister. Well, now was his chance.

"You play games all day at work. You'll be perfect for this." She managed to keep her face straight long enough for Seth's pained look to appear, the same look he got every time she talked about his work. Then she smiled at him and went back into the living room with a glass of water and some crackers and cheese.

With the dogs crated in the other room, Charlotte stopped crying. She leaned on Hannah, a cracker in one hand and a slice of cheese in the other.

Hannah smoothed her daughter's hair from her brow. "Maybe we should move to an area without carpet?"

Waving that worry away, Penelope pulled a chair over. "Trust me, the dogs will take care of any dropped food as soon as they're free again. Don't worry about it. Put your feet up and relax for a bit." She raised an eyebrow as Hannah grimaced and pressed a hand to her swollen belly.

"Braxton Hicks contractions. I'm pretty sure." Hannah sighed. "At least I hope so. The baby's not supposed to be here for another five weeks."

Seth was bringing over another chair. At her words, he paled. "Contractions? I'll call an ambulance."

Penelope grabbed his arm to keep him from dialing. "Relax. Everything's fine. Braxton Hicks contractions are normal. It doesn't mean she's in labor." She sat down, hoping that an outward sign of calm would convince everyone else to relax. "And I'm sure Jake has delivered a baby or two."

Jake looked at her skeptically and sat down in the chair

he'd brought from the kitchen. "You're thinking of fire-fighters."

"You might be right." Penelope eyed him speculatively. "You have such a great body, I must have gotten confused." With a shrug, she turned back to Hannah. "Isn't dehydration the most common cause of Braxton Hicks?" She stared at Hannah's untouched water glass until the other woman started drinking. "Right. Let's get Charlotte settled before we talk."

When the toddler was safely ensconced next to her mother with a tablet showing a cartoon musical and noise-cancelling headphones nearly as large as her head, Hannah seemed to finally relax. "This whole weekend has been such a nightmare."

Penelope nodded sympathetically and forced herself to start at a logical place. "First things first. Does Todd have a criminal attorney, or do we need to arrange that for him?" She inwardly shuddered at the thought of what her ex-husband might say while in custody. Having never been caught up in the criminal justice system, Todd naively assumed people who were innocent would be released with an apology. The only reason he'd hired Jake was to avoid the inconvenience of being arrested and having to clear his name. Penelope doubted Todd had ever considered many people had been convicted on far less evidence than the police had against him.

Jake spoke up. "I gave him the contact info for two attorneys yesterday and told him to keep that on him. He should be set."

Hannah looked between Penelope and Jake, confused. "What? When did you see Todd yesterday?"

Of course that idiot hadn't told his wife he'd hired Jake. Penelope didn't know why she assumed Todd had gotten better at communication in his third marriage. She opened her mouth to answer, then stopped. Ethically, Jake couldn't divulge his client information, even to the client's wife. And while Penelope was an employee of the firm, she couldn't either.

Luckily, she didn't need to say anything. Hannah noted her hesitation. "Oh. Right. Seth mentioned Jake had begun working as a private investigator." She looked at Seth. "That's what this is about, isn't it?"

Seth nodded.

Penelope's train of thought wandered off onto a different track as she considered that Seth clearly talked more to his father's wife than he did to his father. Todd hadn't even known about Jake's retirement. Or he'd been told and hadn't paid attention. Or just forgot. That was entirely possible.

Jake glanced over and cleared his throat, obviously noticing that her mind had wandered. He looked back at Hannah. "Can you tell us exactly what happened?"

Letting out a long, slow breath, Hannah ran a hand over her belly. "We were getting ready to go out to dinner when there was a knock on the door. When I answered it, the police were there — a man and a woman. They had a search warrant."

Jake leaned forward just a bit. "Did you read it?"

She shook her head, looking crestfallen. "I didn't even think to." She looked over at Penelope. "Why didn't I look at it? You would have!"

The comparison rocked Penelope back. "Eight months pregnant and responsible for a small child? Trust me, I would have told them to take whatever they needed and gone back to bed." She turned to Jake. "What's on the search warrant that you wanted to know?" She realized she'd never actually seen a search warrant and was seized by the desire to hold one in her hand.

"Whether it was just the motel room or the car as well.

Both cars." At Penelope's quizzical look, he explained. "This feels... sudden. It's Sunday afternoon, and they found a judge willing to sign off on a search warrant. They must have had something convincing. If the warrant only covered the motel room, that probably means they knew exactly where what they were looking for was."

Penelope thought that over for a few seconds. "As in, someone said 'hey, I saw this bloody axe in this guy's closet' and not 'hey, I saw that guy running away from the crime scene with a bloody axe'?"

"Exactly. If they only had information about a weapon in the motel room, the judge wouldn't sign off on a search of the cars." He tilted his head. "Probably. Depends on the judge."

Hannah held her empty glass in both hands. "But why does that matter?"

Giving in to her desire to move, Penelope stood and retrieved Hannah's glass. "Let me guess," she said as she walked toward the kitchen, automatically raising her voice so she'd be heard over the distance. "We know Todd was in the area when both murders happened, so if the search warrant included the cars, it would suggest they found security video or something like that." She paused to refill Hannah's glass, then walked back into the living room. "But if someone tipped the police off that there was a weapon in the room, the warrant would only cover the room."

Handing the glass to Hannah, Penelope sighed. "So there really *might* be someone trying to frame the weasel." Then she remembered Hannah was still married to Todd. "I shouldn't have called him that. Not that there's anything wrong with weasels, of course. You have to love anything where a group of them is called a confusion." She sat down again, hoping Hannah wouldn't notice her clarification hadn't actually made her words nicer. After more than fifty years of putting her foot in her mouth, Penelope had learned that sometimes it was just better to stop talking.

"I didn't see anyone going through Todd's car, and they didn't stop us from leaving with the minivan." Hannah halted with the glass halfway to her lips. "But why would someone want to frame *Todd*?"

Penelope kept her mouth shut with an effort. Back when she'd been in the middle of divorcing the man, she'd had days where she'd needed to convince herself that murdering him was a bad solution. Setting him up to go to prison for someone else's crime would have seemed almost honorable compared to that.

Jake's mouth twitched, as if he knew exactly what she was thinking. "I think the most likely answer would be: because he was in the right place at the right time, at least for the first murder. And then he was lured to the right place for the second crime." He shrugged. "There are other possibilities, of course. Someone he's in business with, or anyone who has a personal grudge against him..."

Hannah attempted a laugh. "I think I'm the only one with a grudge against him at the moment."

The bristles of his five o'clock shadow made a noise like sandpaper on wood as Jake rubbed his chin. "You underestimate how long some people can hold a grudge." He turned his head to look at Penelope, who batted her lashes at him innocently.

Seth muffled a laugh.

Suddenly, Hannah looked uncertain again. "I should go. If Todd has a lawyer, there's nothing more I can do here. It's not that long of a drive to get home." She shifted her weight forward, as if preparing to heave herself to her feet.

Penelope stood up to forestall her. "Nonsense. Hannah, you're in no shape to drive tonight. And you'd just have to drive back again tomorrow for the arraignment." Todd might have been ready to give up on his marriage, but Hannah wasn't; she'd want to be there when her husband went in front of the judge. "Seth, go put clean sheets on the guest room bed. You can have the couch in the office tonight. Did you bring a play yard for Charlotte to sleep in? Give me your car keys. Jake and I will get it out of the van."

Hannah blinked. "But..."

"Keys?" Penelope held out her hand.

Seth stood up. "Just let her take care of you. Once she gets like this, there's no point arguing."

"But..." Hannah looked at her daughter, who was engrossed in the movie, thumb in her mouth. "Thank you."

"That's that, then." Penelope took the offered keys and headed for the door. Now all they had to do was figure out who had killed two people so they could get Todd out of jail in time to witness the birth of his new child.

.

CHAPTER 20

*P*enelope left Jake and Seth to ply Hannah and Charlotte with food. Finding a murderer was important, but she still had pet sitting clients to take care of. In this case, that meant dinner, medication, and a walk around the block for a Labrador named Harvey, whose owners were gone for the weekend, followed by an extended cuddling and clean-up session for the four cats owned by a friend of Esther who was in the hospital with a broken hip. In the meantime, maybe Jake would learn something new from Hannah.

Flopped on the couch with four cats draped over her, *One Wild Night* propped on her chest, Penelope struggled to stay awake. Her eyes kept skipping over whole paragraphs of tedious internal monologue. "I have my doubts about this book," she said to Hera, the long-haired orange cat draped over one arm. "Maybe there's a metaphor I'm missing." Hera blinked and closed her eyes.

Penelope's phone rang, and she partially dislodged two cats in getting it out of her pocket. Not a number she recognized, but clients sometimes called from other phones. "You've reached Penelope!"

"Penelope, this is Roberta Stacks. We met earlier today?"

Penelope would have recognized the voice even if the other woman hadn't given her name. "Of course! Is everything okay?"

"Yes. Sorry to call so late, but you didn't strike me as someone who would be in bed at eight."

"This is fine. I'm actually at a client's house relaxing with the cats." Penelope thought back to their earlier conversation. "If you read that entire book since I saw you, I need you to tell me your speed reading secrets."

Laughter came from the phone. "Nothing so impressive. But I did find my notes from when I was putting the course together. I marked two chapters where the writing seemed different from the rest of the book."

Penelope flipped through the hardback in front of her. "Let me guess. One is chapter... twelve?" In that section, two teenagers were picked up by the politician in the bar and taken to his room. The scene closely matched Lenz's memories, at least until the book's characters arrived at the suite.

"Indeed. Any guesses on the second?"

"Not a clue."

"Chapter fifty-four, where the couple sabotage a car when they're on the run."

Penelope flipped forward, searching for chapter fifty-four. When Hera batted at the moving paper with one fluffy orange paw, Penelope shifted the novel out of the way. "Don't damage the library book."

"Sorry?"

"Talking to the cat." She found the right chapter and marked it with a corner torn off her bookmark. "Thanks for letting me know. I hadn't gotten that far yet and I don't know if I would notice the writing being different."

"I remember I read over it a few times because I wasn't sure if the language had changed, or if I was just knocked out of the narrative because the action matched something that had happened to a colleague of mine."

"Really?" Penelope forced herself to concentrate on the conversation by closing the book — it had transitioned from inner monologues to an action scene that looked a whole lot more interesting. "Did they get hurt?"

"She died, actually. Drove off the side of the road into a ravine." Before Penelope could offer any condolences, Roberta continued quickly. "She wasn't a close friend. I mostly knew her from faculty meetings. I suppose we might have supported each other, but I kept my distance because she slept with the young men in her classes. The male faculty do that sort of thing regularly and accuse me of being a prude when I object. It's amazing how quickly they find it offensive when a woman does the same thing."

Roberta gave an exasperated snort. "She left before anything could be proven, and the university swept it under the rug as it always does. But that's neither here nor there. She had taken a non-tenured position at another college by the time she died. When they examined the car, most of the lug nuts had been removed from the wheels and the brakes had been tampered with. This was... oh, maybe five, ten years ago. There was a lot of news coverage — I assume that's where Ms. Webb got the idea."

Penelope struggled to sit up, displacing four disgruntled cats. "Did they find the person who did it?"

"I don't think so. Most of what I remember is all the hysteria from my fellow faculty about whether it was safe to give students poor grades. But it was far more likely to have been done by a spouse or lover than a failing student."

"True." Penelope thought about this new information as she rubbed her face. Her recent late nights were catching up with her. "Do you remember your colleague's name?" Maybe Lenz would know if Ashley had some connection with the woman.

"Edie Glaspell. The head of the department called her 'Speedy Edie' because of the length of her relationships, which only goes to show that misogyny is alive and well in the higher institutions of learning. Meanwhile, the department head was in his sixties and his wife was a twenty-five-year-old grad student who did all the work for his undergrad classes."

Penelope scratched Hera's chin. "Is it like a soap opera at every college?"

"Ha!" Roberta's bark of laughter made Penelope move the phone away from her ear. "More often than not! You'd be surprised." Ice cubes clinked against glass. "I'll let you get on with your evening. Call me if you have any questions."

"Thank you." Penelope disconnected and looked at the thick chunk of pages between her spot in the book and chapter fifty-four. "I'll just skip to that part and come back and read the rest later if I have time."

Hera rubbed her cheek against the book as Penelope settled down to read.

CHAPTER 21

*B*ack at home, things had quieted. Hannah and Charlotte had gone to bed, Seth had moved to Jake's office to play a game with his online friends, and Jake sat at the end of the couch with a golf tournament on the television. Brutus sprawled next to him, and Frodo had taken up his accustomed position on the back of the couch near Jake's shoulder.

Sliding in next to Jake with a tray of jalapeño poppers balanced on her library book, Penelope handed him a glass of wine. Brutus raised his head at the smell of cheese but quickly looked away when she frowned at him. "Have I ever told you what an amazing man you are?"

"You didn't sign me up to mulch the rose gardens again, did you?"

"No. Though I can't swear Esther hasn't." Penelope bit into deep-fried pepper and mozzarella and groaned. "We should crash wedding receptions more often. If we plan it right, we'll never have to cook again."

"Because we'll both drop dead from the cholesterol within six months."

"Maybe. But it will be a great six months." Penelope savored the other half of the popper before circling back to her point. "I just wanted to thank you for letting Hannah and Charlotte stay here tonight. Some men would complain if their wife's ex-husband's current wife and child showed up."

"I like Hannah. She can stay anytime." He sipped his wine. "Fair warning: if she goes into labor, I'll drive to the hospital, but you're responsible for handling anything that happens along the way."

Penelope grinned and turned her head to kiss his cheek. "Deal."

"How's the book?"

"I think Ashley spent too much time reading *A Catcher in the Rye*. But Roberta called and gave me some hints. She said the writing changed in the chapter where the politician meets the teenagers, which we know from Lenz actually happened. And it changes again in chapter fifty-four."

"And what happens in chapter fifty-four?"

Penelope handed him the plate, wiped her fingers on the napkin, and flipped open the book. "This is the section where they go on a crime spree after the politician dies. It's a little *Thelma & Louise*, except with teenagers and one's a boy. And without a real reason for what they're doing." She paused to think about it. "So, really, nothing like *Thelma & Louise*. That was a bad analogy."

"I think I get the picture." He glanced at the book and drew his head back. "When did they start making the font so big?"

"The only one not checked out was the large print version." Penelope considered the book in her lap. "You know, if I'm being totally honest, this *is* actually easier to read."

"I promise I won't tell anyone." He took another look at

the book and turned back to the golf with a quick shake of his head. "So what happens?"

"I skimmed the chapter before I left the cats. The kids decide to get back at their math teacher by loosening the wheels on his car and messing with the brakes. He's a perv who's been pressuring the girl to come to him for 'extra tutoring' all year, so I don't know, I could maybe make a case that it's justified, but if we were on the run after accidentally killing a man, would you want to go back and settle a score with your high school math teacher?"

Jake clicked the tip of his tongue against the back of his front teeth. "That would be difficult since Mr. Palmer died about twenty years ago."

"Sure, but even so."

"Somehow I doubt the character motivations are what Roberta wanted you to notice." He waved the plate under her face. "Focus."

Penelope ate another popper and wiped her fingers again. "Seriously, the death by cholesterol thing is going to be worth it." She flipped the page. "Okay, so we have a section here where there's a pretty detailed description of the kids loosening the lug nuts. But they aren't sure that will be enough, so they also do something to the brakes. That part is a little less technical. I get the feeling Ashley didn't know any more about cars than I do, though I'd believe she watched someone else do it." She flipped the book closed and took the plate back from him. "But Roberta *also* said that she thought Ashley had gotten the idea from real life. A professor died when her car was sabotaged and she drove off a cliff."

"Ashley might just have heard about it, but maybe she had a connection to this other professor. Did you find out her name?"

"Yes." There was a long pause.

Jake turned his head and raised one brow. "You didn't write it down."

Penelope winced. "It rhymed, so I thought I'd remember. And I didn't have anything to write with."

"Except your phone."

"I never remember I can type notes on my phone for stuff like that." Penelope rested her head against his shoulder and closed her eyes. "Hang on. Let me think. It was something like 'Loosey Goosey.'"

"The professor's last name was Goosey?"

"No, it was her first name."

"Her *first* name is Goosey?" The disbelief in his voice inspired Frodo to give an enquiring bark.

Penelope opened her eyes and stuck out her tongue at Jake. "Early Shirley? Meanie Jeanie?"

"I'll call Roberta in the morning and ask." He leaned over to kiss her temple.

The last guess knocked some dust off her brain cells. "Speedy Edie. Ha! I knew I'd remember. Her name was Edie."

"Edie..." Jake waited.

"Oh, yeah, there's no way I'd remember the last name. But we might be able to figure it out. Edie's not a common first name and the crash made it into the papers." Jake had his phone out before she could lean over to reach hers. "Hang on, I'm not ready to start yet."

He nudged her phone farther away with one foot and his fingers sped up. "It's not a race."

Penelope rested her forearm on his thigh so she could reach her phone. Unlocking it and bringing up the tiny browser seemed to take forever. She had just typed in "Edie car crash", when Jake triumphantly held his phone out in front of her.

"Too slow. You can't beat my magic hands. Edie Glaspell."

"Cheater."

"Hey, I wasn't the one who knew the name and forgot it in the first place. You're just jealous *you* don't have magic hands." He extended his arm and drew his head back while he scanned the article. "Doesn't look like they ever charged anyone. As far as the car, it just says both the brakes and the wheels were tampered with, in a 'deliberate act of sabotage'. No specifics."

"So this may or may not have anything to do with Ashley."

"True." Jake checked a few more articles before putting his phone down on the arm of the couch near Frodo. "When you were hindering Seth's search of Ashley's social media accounts, did you see any mention of Lone Pine College?"

"Ha! Shows what you know. I didn't hinder his search at all." Penelope didn't mention that Seth had mailed her the links. "Is that where Edie was teaching when she died? I've never even heard of it."

"It's a few hours northeast of here. I drove up there once to retrieve some stolen property."

Penelope shifted so she could look at him more clearly. "*You* went to retrieve stolen property." That was a task generally left to the owner, or maybe a junior detective if there was some extenuating circumstance.

"Had to pay up on a debt. I owed the chief of their campus police a bottle of scotch. But it gave me an excuse to bring back the stolen statue before we got any more bad press."

"Ah," Penelope said, understanding. Now she knew exactly what the stolen property was. The statue of the town's founder stood in the park less than one block from the police station. About six years before, a group of students had analyzed a weakness in the way it had been mounted. They'd come back with a stolen tow truck, and while two men had staged a drunken brawl in a nearby bar to draw the graveyard shift patrol officers, the rest of the group had shattered the bolts and driven away with the statue.

Because of the location near the police station and because the statue had been executed by a local artist with more zeal than ability, the caper had hit the national newspapers. For three days, reporters had extended the story by highlighting the artist's other works, which included a poorly executed bust of the founder's daughter, and a truly terrible rendition of her beagle. Penelope was fond of Rex's statue, as were many others based on the shiny patch on his head where everyone stooped to pet him. But even Penelope had to admit Rex didn't look anything like a beagle. Or even a dog, really.

Back to the matter at hand. "I don't see how Ashley would be connected to Lone Pine College. Unless maybe she met one of Edie's students." She let her phone drop onto the sofa next to her leg, which left her hand free to pick up the last popper. "Roberta said Edie left the college here because she got caught dating undergrads. I don't suppose any newspaper article lists the students in her class when she died."

"No, but we'll have to go through everyone involved to see if they have any connections to Lone Pine College." Jake stretched his back. "Tomorrow."

"Tomorrow," Penelope agreed. She got to her feet. "Are you and your magic hands coming to bed now, or should I put some blankets on the floor so you don't have to worry about disturbing Frodo later?"

"When you put it that way..." He tapped the remote, and the television went dark. "I'd hate to let my magic hands go to waste."

Penelope gave him a quelling look. "Pause that thought until we don't have an easily woken toddler and a loud and possessive chihuahua in the house."

He stood and faced her, clasping his hands behind her waist. "We could always go to a hotel."

"Or a vacation rental." Penelope leaned forward and

pecked his cheek. "Let's just figure out how to get the devil out of jail so he can go back home with his wife. Then we can work on figuring out where the chihuahua belongs."

"Incentive." Jake let his arms drop. "You go on up. I'll lock up the house. Don't let Frodo hog the bed before I get there."

CHAPTER 22

No matter what else happened on Monday morning, there was always solace in the ritual of going to church. Or, not exactly the church, but the rectory kitchen to relax with Spot while CJ held weekday services. The shabby surroundings inspired comfort, as did the stale pastry, and having her husband seated on the floor next to her. The graying Dalmatian draped over their legs slapped her tail against the floor as Penelope stroked her ears.

Jake scrolled through his phone. "The court schedule isn't up yet, but unless they've changed things recently, Todd's arraignment should be at ten o'clock. You're still scheduled to deliver mail this morning, right?"

"Yes." She made a face. "I'm stuck on the new house route." The new houses at the east end of town had been built for efficiency; instead of individual boxes in front of every house, a bank of lockers stood at the end of each cul-de-sac. Most of the mail carriers preferred it because it required less walking. Penelope hated it. "Maybe I should call in sick. Hannah shouldn't be alone."

Jake cleared his throat. "You may not be the best person to

go to court with her. Remember, the point is to make sure Todd isn't sitting in jail when the baby is born. Having you two glaring at each other across the courtroom isn't going to convince the judge that Todd is safe on the streets."

Penelope considered arguing purely out of principle, but he was right. "I could wear a disguise."

"I'll go with her. Seth can watch Charlotte at home. He's a familiar face, so maybe she'll be okay with that." He paused to take a sip of coffee. "And the dogs are there."

Penelope snorted. The biggest surprise of the morning had been that both dogs adored the toddler, and now that she'd had some sleep, the toddler adored them back. Charlotte had bolted out of the spare bedroom before Penelope could crate the dogs. Brutus had gone into a play bow in front of her, then run off to retrieve his stuffed badger and drop it in front of the child. That made Penelope relax; Brutus only offered the stuffed badger to people he liked, and he could be careful with his bulk when he wanted to, as evidenced by the fact that he hadn't stepped on Frodo yet. For his part, the chihuahua sat down next to the girl every time she settled in one place. Someone still needed to watch their interactions closely, but the development made the house more peaceful.

She absently ate the last piece of bear claw while considering the effort it would take to keep a straight face as Todd spoke to the judge. Maybe it *would* be better if she delivered mail instead.

Jake looked at the empty plate, then set it down with a sigh. "It's weird how quickly I eat those things. And I don't even remember doing it."

"Just a touch of dementia." Penelope patted his shoulder. "Don't worry. I'll put you in a nice home before I go on a cruise with the rest of your money."

He laughed as he carefully slid Spot off his legs so he

could get up. "As if you could sit still long enough to go on a cruise. You'd be pacing holes into the deck and telling the captain to drive faster. More coffee?"

"No, thanks. I'm good."

"Pretty sure the jury's still out on that." He folded himself back into place with another bear claw on his plate.

Penelope eyed the pastry. Jake's recent talk of cholesterol had convinced her she should eat more healthy food, but perhaps that could wait until tomorrow. They would eat salads when all their guests had left. She broke off a chunk. "Fine. We'll do it your way. This will give Seth and Charlotte a chance to get to know each other."

"The way things are going, Seth might be the only male role model Charlotte has."

"True." Penelope leaned against his warm shoulder, enjoying being near this man who knew her so well. "I just want to grab Todd by the shoulders and shake him until he grows up. Hannah and Charlotte deserve better than that."

"Maybe spending a night in jail will force him to think about what's important."

"Maybe." She tore off another corner of the pastry and enjoyed the gritty texture of sweetened almond filling. "I'm staying out of it." When Jake laughed quietly, she elbowed him. "No, really. If it looks like I'm wading in, pull the fire alarm or something."

"Right."

Penelope ignored the doubt in his voice. "I'm going to spend some time online trying to find any connection between Ashley and Lone Pine College. How about you?"

"Lenz is coming to the house this afternoon to go over his list of high school friends or anyone else who might have known about the photos. And if I have time before court, I'll see if I still know anyone at the Lone Pine campus police.

Maybe I can get a peek at their suspect list in the Glaspell case."

Penelope rubbed Spot's ear, setting the elderly dog's tail wagging again. "Fingers crossed something in this mess points to someone other than Todd. Otherwise, you might have to become Hannah's Lamaze coach." She looked at his nearly empty plate. "Though the breathing exercises might help you burn off all those carbs."

CHAPTER 23

a last-minute switch had Penelope delivering mail on a route that included the downtown businesses and a swath of older houses. Since the business deliveries mostly entailed going inside and handing the mail to a person, she held off on making calls to people who had known Ashley more recently, like her agent and dog walker.

Convincing them to talk to a total stranger about Ashley's connection to Lone Pine would require all of Penelope's concentration. But the random bits of information gleaned from her deliveries were too much of a lure to be ignored.

Ronald the florist received a hand-lettered envelope holding a single sheet with feminine writing on the outside but no name, which suggested he'd picked up another penpal. Postmarked in New Zealand this time. As usual, Ronald quickly shoved the missive under the counter. From his reaction, it might have been a pornographic magazine. As far as Penelope knew, Ronald was gay, which made the whole thing even more intriguing. Someday, she hoped to find out what that was all about, but she merely nodded hello and continued on her path.

The state assemblyman had an office above an antique store, though Penelope had only seen him there once. Usually she only saw his local staff, which consisted entirely of Gabriela, a Latina in her thirties who enhanced her pay by translating romance novels into Spanish after she finished her daily tasks. The reception job required her to wait in case someone walked in, but not many people knew about the office, so Gabriela rarely had much to do. When both she and Penelope had free time, they critiqued the sex scenes in whatever manuscript Gabriela was working on.

On this day, though, men's voices came from the closed office behind Gabriela's desk. Penelope handed over a stack of mail and took a stack in return. "Sounds like the boss is here."

Gabriela kept her voice low. "I wish he would go. I'm running out of things to do to look busy."

"Reorganize the filing cabinets," Penelope suggested as she tapped her index finger on her nose.

"I did that on Friday."

Penelope thought about Seth's complaints. "Upgrade all your software. That will take at least a few days, and it probably needs to be done anyhow."

Before Gabriela could reply, the door behind her opened, and three men in suits came out. The oldest one Penelope vaguely recognized from prior election mailers as the assemblyman. The second man she didn't know. But the third man saw her, and his eyes gleamed. Kieran Engle shook the second man's hand while smiling widely. "If I haven't gotten back to you by Wednesday, give me a call. You have my number, correct?"

"I do." He shook the assemblyman's hand. "Watch out for this one, Lenny. He'll be running for your spot one of these days."

"Don't I know it." The office hadn't been built for such

hearty chuckles, and the window panes rattled. He turned and went back into his office; the unknown man headed for the staircase.

Kieran moved around the reception desk. "If it isn't the only person who beat me on Saturday night! How are you doing, Ms. Standing? You here to talk to the assemblyman?" His grip was warm and firm, and Penelope found herself agreeing with the man who had just left. With his good looks and ability to remember people and names, Kieran would go far in the political scene.

"Fine, thanks." She tugged at the mail bag slung over her right hip. "Just delivering the mail." She waved to both Kieran and Gabriela, then stopped mid-turn. "While I have you here... Do you know if Ashley had any connection to Lone Pine College?"

Kieran cocked his head. "Where?"

"Lone Pine College. It's..." She looked around to orient herself, then pointed north. "Thataway. A few hours."

Shaking his head, Kieran said, "Not that I know of. I don't think Ashley ever went to any college." His brows drew down. "I thought they arrested someone for the murders yesterday — the old guy who was hitting on her at the reception."

Penelope tried to keep the grimace off her face. "I'm pretty sure my ex-husband didn't do it."

Gabriela was suddenly fascinated with something on her desk. Kieran nodded slowly. "Ah."

Penelope patted her mail bag. "Well, I should get going. Have a nice day!" She trotted down the stairs, wondering if she could have possibly made the moment any more awkward.

The used bookstore at the corner didn't have any mail, but Penelope ducked in anyhow so she could pet the store cat, a gray Persian. When the bell over the door rang,

Mephistopheles lifted his head from his usual spot on top of the bookcase near the register. The smell of old paper, oil paint, jasmine incense, and a hint of marijuana hadn't changed in the thirty years since Penelope had first found the store. No humans were visible, but that wasn't uncommon. Barbara had a studio in the back where she painted re-imagined fantasy scenes in the style of pulp covers from the 1920s. Collectors paid enough to keep the quiet bookstore in business.

"It's just me, Barbara," Penelope called out. Mephistopheles purred as Penelope cleaned the crusts away from his eyes.

Barbara's voice floated in from the studio. "Need help finding anything?"

"No, I just came in to see Mephi." The cat rubbed his cheek against her fingers. Then Penelope remembered her other bit of book news and she pitched her voice to be heard in the studio. "Did you know E. E. Cummings wrote a book of erotic poetry?"

Barbara laughed. "Seth did it justice at the wedding."

Penelope moved her fingers over to Mephi's ears. She whispered to the cat, "You and I are in the cool club of people who didn't get invited." He purred more loudly. Penelope raised her voice again. "I missed the ceremony, but at least I got some food from the reception."

"Best of both worlds." Barbara's voice got closer, and she rounded the corner, a streak of ochre going from her cheekbone into her long gray hair. Her smock showed evidence of other earth tones being used in the current painting. "I think we have the Cummings in the erotic poetry section, unless Darla sold it while I was out. Stacked on top of the romance aisle," she added, before Penelope could ask. Barbara caught sight of her reflection in the glass covering her business license. "How did that...?" Grabbing a rag from her back pocket, she wiped the paint off her face, depositing more in her hair. "I thought leaving the character's shirt off was a good idea three days ago. Do you know how many muscles there are in a man's back?"

Assuming that was a rhetorical question, Penelope wandered down the packed romance aisle. The genre took up a quarter of the shop's space, and would have been even larger if so many avid romance readers hadn't switched to ebooks. Barbara had split up the paperbacks by type, from "lgbtq+" near the floor to "guy next door" at eye level and "taboo" on the shelf above. With the constant turnover, Penelope always found something before she got to the end, so it wasn't a surprise that she'd missed the "romantic & erotic poetry" section nestled under the exposed beams. She pulled over the nearby footstool and found the book she was looking for, a slim white volume labeled "erotic poems" in a tasteful red font.

On the way back to the front counter, Penelope glimpsed the high school yearbooks stacked in the corner. Seth had gone to the public high school, but he'd thrown out his yearbooks when Penelope had lost her house. She found one from Ashley's graduating class and brought it to Barbara, along with the poetry book.

Barbara raised one orange and gray eyebrow. "Seth doesn't have his?"

"He got rid of it a while back. I thought I might find out who Ashley Webb was friends with in high school." Paging through the index for any mention of Ashley, Penelope got sidetracked by Seth's entry. She flipped back to the section on clubs and saw him leaning over a table covered in cards and plastic counters, with a group of kids also standing and staring at the contents. "They were so young then."

Barbara snorted as she rang up Penelope's purchases. "They still are."

"True." Penelope closed the yearbook and dug cash from her pocket. "It's a good thing, too. He can handle getting up in the middle of the night when the toddler has a nightmare and needs someone to read books to her." Catching Barbara's quizzical look, she shook her head. "His half-sister. My ex's current wife and her baby are staying with us for a bit."

Barbara nodded without batting an eye. "Family. Give everyone my best."

CHAPTER 24

A text from Jake told Penelope that Todd had been released on bail, so she wasn't surprised to hear her ex-husband's voice when she went home for a late lunch. Brutus and Frodo ran to greet her, but their sniffing seemed perfunctory. Then they turned around and ran back into the kitchen, from which Penelope deduced someone was slipping them food under the table.

She was half right — the table was clear of food, but Charlotte's high chair held pieces of what had once been a peanut butter and jelly sandwich. The toddler shrieked and squirmed away from the washcloth Seth held, flinging her arms out. Frodo leaped in front of Brutus's open jaws to grab the morsel that fell.

At the table, Todd sat with his phone pressed to one ear, his hand clapped over the other ear to block out the chaos. "What do you mean there's no record of it? It's not something you could misplace... Fine, what's the number... No, don't transfer me back to the main menu, wait!" He put the phone down with a scowl. "They hung up on me again. How can they impound my car and lose it?"

Penelope ignored him and dropped a kiss on the cleanest part of Charlotte's head. "Hannah is...?"

"Taking a nap," Seth answered as he wiped Charlotte's hand. "And Jake went for a run with that German shepherd."

Darn the man. Taking Heidi for a run had been the excuse *she* had been planning to use to escape the house for a while.

Seth kept a straight face. "He said he'd apologize later."

"There's no need. He's helping with the business." At least she had other pet sitting clients that might need an extra check-in or two during the day.

"Uh huh." Seth lifted Charlotte up and handed her to Penelope so he could clean the high chair tray.

Penelope lifted the baby, sniffed twice, and walked over to Todd. "Your daughter needs a new diaper." She narrowed her eyes at him when he opened his mouth to say something. "You know perfectly well how to change a diaper, so if you're claiming otherwise, I'll drive you back to jail myself and tell them you're planning on fleeing the country."

"That's not what..." Todd turned his daughter around so she was sitting on his lap. "I don't know where the diaper bag is. I've been trying to find out what happened to my car since I got here."

"It's next to the sofa in the living room," Seth said.

Penelope took the high chair tray from her son's hands. "Come on, you two," she called to the dogs. They followed her to the yard, and she left them outside to lick it clean. "Changing a toddler's diaper is hard enough," she said, at Seth's raised eyebrow. "Adding two dogs into the mix isn't necessary. Besides, I don't want them fighting over the diaper."

"Ugh."

"You have to think ahead about these things." She opened the refrigerator and inhaled the mingled scents. "Say what you want about that wedding, but they had great food." As she piled appetizers on a plate, she glanced at Seth. "Aren't you supposed to be at work today?"

"I told my boss I had a family emergency."

If your father getting arrested for murder didn't count as a family emergency, Penelope didn't know what did. She lowered her voice. "So, what's the deal with the car?"

Seth shrugged. "Hannah and Jake dropped Dad off at the motel after the arraignment, and by the time he'd finished packing, his car was gone. Jake thought they might have impounded it to look for more evidence, but nobody knows what department would have it."

Jake would know who to ask. So either he had offered to find out and been ignored, or Todd had irritated him enough that Jake hadn't offered. He would probably still make the calls to find out.

The doorbell rang. Penelope shoved off the chair to her feet. "Don't eat all my lunch while I'm gone."

With the dogs in the backyard, answering the door was a shorter process. "Brianna, Jake's not here, but he should be back soon. Come on in." Then Penelope stopped as she took in the other woman's stance, and the two uniformed patrol officers behind her. "Or is it Detective Sanchez today?"

There had been a time when the appearance of uniformed officers on her doorstep would have caused panic. But Jake was retired now, and she was pretty sure Brianna's visit wasn't related to him.

"Is your ex-husband here, Ms. Standing?"

Penelope sighed. Witnessing the arrest of her ex-husband for a serious crime had been on her wishlist for at least a decade after they'd split up — not because she thought he was guilty of anything, but because she just wanted to see him in a situation he couldn't talk his way out of. But that dream had faded long ago, and she certainly didn't want the event to take place in her own house while a small child and a very pregnant woman were present. "He's changing the baby's diaper at the moment. Let me get him for you."

Then she shut the door.

When she turned around, Todd's face had gone white.

Penelope raised her voice so she'd be heard in the kitchen. "Seth, can you take Charlotte for a bit?"

Todd took a shaky breath. "I just got out of there. Why would they be here for me again?" He finished pulling on Charlotte's tights and stood up, cradling the girl protectively against his side. "This can't be happening. I can't go back."

There were lines on his face that hadn't been there the day before, and for the first time that week, he looked his age. His eyes darted from the front door to the room where Hannah slept. Then he swallowed and squared his shoulders. He kissed Charlotte's forehead. "Be good for Seth, okay, Charlie-bunny?" As he handed her over to his son, he cleared his throat. "Take her somewhere she won't see this. Please."

Seth nodded and looked down at the girl in his arms. "You ready to help me teach the unicorn how to fly? I have an extra controller without batteries, just for you. Let's go." He walked toward Jake's office. Charlotte watched her father over Seth's shoulder, looking uncertain. Remembering how quickly small children picked up on moods, Penelope forced herself to smile and wave.

After Seth and Charlotte were no longer in sight, Penelope stooped to clean up the diaper-changing supplies, then halted when Todd held up a hand. "No. Let me take care of my own mess." He paused. "Technically, Charlotte's mess, but you know what I mean." He drew a long breath. "I'm going to finish here, wash my hands, call my lawyer, and then find out why the police are after me for the second time in two days."

Penelope nodded and didn't point out it sounded like he was trying to convince himself. "Good plan." She plucked the plastic bag holding the tightly rolled used diaper from his hand. "But it's probably better if you don't head out back to put this in the trash can right now. That might be seen as an attempt to flee."

He made an attempt to smile. "Your monster dog would knock me down and stand on top of me if I tried."

As much as she wanted to defend Brutus, Penelope thought Todd might be right about that. At least the knocking down part. Around Charlotte, the mastiff moved in slow motion, placing each foot carefully so he didn't bump into her. But Brutus sometimes forgot how big he was when faced with an adult.

Fifteen minutes later, Penelope was standing next to the silent Detective Sanchez watching a hand-cuffed Todd being put in the back seat of the police car when Jake arrived. He was still sweaty from the run, but Penelope ignored that and gave him a fierce hug. "I have no idea what's going on," she murmured. Then she forced herself to turn around and go back inside. It killed Penelope to leave when interesting things were happening, but Jake would get more information out of Brianna if she wasn't around.

By the time Jake came in ten minutes later, Penelope, Seth, Charlotte, and both dogs were waiting in the living room. Penelope tried to wait until the dogs had finished sniffing, but she was too impatient. "Did you find out what's going on?"

Jake nodded, looking grave. "Someone ran down Lenz Russell today. A hit and run, and it looked deliberate. He's in surgery now."

"But why would they think Todd did it?"

"Because whoever did it was driving Todd's car."

CHAPTER 25

*P*enelope, Jake, and Seth sat on the grass in the backyard, Charlotte sucking her thumb and leaning on her half-brother. Jake pushed Brutus's head out of the way so he could see Penelope. "The problem is, he *could* have done it."

Penelope shook her head stubbornly. "There's no way Todd deliberately ran down someone in his car. He's obsessive about his cars." Todd had never needed to own anything flashy, but his vehicles were always in immaculate condition, from the day he bought them until the day the mileage was high enough it made more sense to buy a new one.

Seth groaned. "I dinged his door once and I'm pretty sure he still hasn't forgiven me."

"I'll bet Charlotte hasn't even been *in* that car."

Brutus shoved harder until he was leaning his body on Jake's torso. Jake merely used one hand to brace himself and the other to scratch Brutus's chest. "I didn't say he did it. I said he *could* have done it. The timing was perfect. Hannah and I dropped him off at the motel office to collect his things and came back here. He showed up two hours later.

He had enough time to run down Lenz, dump the car, and get back."

They considered that as Frodo patrolled the edge of the yard, lifting his leg every few inches. With a bladder the size of a walnut, he was fighting a losing battle against the torrent Brutus regularly unleashed. Penelope silently wished the little dog luck and turned back to the conversation. "This bolsters his claim that someone was trying to frame him. Using his car, waiting until he was released from jail..." She fell silent as the logistics sank in. When she looked at Jake, he was watching her, as if he'd heard her thoughts. "No way."

"She could have," Jake said with the hint of a shrug.

Seth looked back and forth at them. "Who could have?"

Penelope spoke before Jake could — Seth wasn't going to take this idea well, and better that it came from her. "Hannah." She held up a hand to forestall his reaction. "I'm not saying she did, but she'd have a key for his car, and she knew when he was released." She turned to Jake, who had almost disappeared under the bulk of the dog. "Did she go out after you came home?"

"She went to the store to pick up diapers and cereal." Jake collapsed onto the grass, letting Brutus finish wiggling his body completely on top of him. "The timing would have been tight, but she could have done it if she'd planned for it." His voice was a little breathless from the dog's bulk, but he didn't sound convinced.

"It's not possible," Seth said, anger coloring his words. "Hannah would *never* do something like that."

Penelope let him off the hook. "I agree. For two reasons." She held up a finger. "One, this was planned, and Hannah would never risk the baby." She held up a second finger. "And two, if she was going to kill someone, she would have started with Todd. Trust me on that." Pregnant, caring for a toddler, and watching her husband flirt with another woman — if

Hannah had run Todd down with her minivan, no jury of women would have convicted her.

"She's at the bottom of the list." Jake's voice was muffled by Brutus's chest, which was now on top of Jake's face.

"I thought *I* was at the bottom of the list."

Jake turned his head to the side so he could see her. "Really?"

Penelope grinned, perversely delighted that her husband had given her a higher spot. "You're right. I knew when the arraignment was, and nobody would have noticed if I'd taken a break from delivering the mail."

"I'd have you even higher up if you had a motive to run down Lenz. And if you had the car key — last time I checked, you hadn't added hot-wiring cars to your resume."

"Do you know anyone who could teach me?" She caught Seth's look of panic and smiled at her husband. "We can talk about that later. I might not have needed it, in this case. Todd used to keep a spare in one of those key holders that sticks to the car frame. Does he still?"

Seth shrugged. "I didn't even know he ever did."

And that, Penelope thought, was entirely Todd's fault. When Seth had first been learning how to drive, Todd had reneged on half the weekends he was supposed to have custody, so Penelope had been the one to teach their son. Given her attitude about following rules, it wasn't a surprise when he'd failed the first driving test.

Now Todd was bungling his third attempt at a family. But even Penelope couldn't believe that leaving him in jail was better than having him out on the streets.

"We'll have to ask Hannah when she wakes up. About the car key," Penelope clarified. "Not whether she ran over Lenz."

Jake pushed Brutus onto the grass and sat up. "I want to know why the killer targeted Lenz today. What changed?

Lenz had already paid the blackmail once, and probably would again. Killing him is literally killing the cash cow."

Penelope tried to keep her mind on the question, but she went off into the weeds picturing a cow with dollar bills falling from its udder as it walked across a pasture. In her image, the cow had a swirl of longer hair on its forehead that stuck up just like Lenz's hair did. Except that couldn't be what the term *cash cow* really meant. Maybe it came from the cash that could be exchanged for a cow. She added it to the list of things to look up at a convenient time, then promptly forgot about it. "They might have realized Lenz had hired you to find them."

"Which gives them a motive to run *me* down. Or you, if they saw you and Brutus following that drone." Jake sighed. "I suppose it's no use asking you to be extra careful for a while."

"You can always ask." A thought struck her. "I asked Kieran about Lone Pine this morning."

Jake sat up straighter. "Really?"

"If he killed Edie and Lenz knew about it, that would explain why Lenz was targeted now. It has to be Kieran."

Seth groaned. "Except this morning, I asked Emma and David if Ashley had ever been to Lone Pine. And half the wedding party was there."

Jake leaned back with a sigh.

Penelope leaned forward to kiss his cheek, then got to her feet. "Hang on, I went to the used bookstore today."

She jogged into the house and returned with her purchases. The slim book of poetry went to Jake with a wink. The yearbook went to Seth. "I thought maybe you could call some of your friends from high school and see if anyone remembers who Ashley hung out with. I still think this all started with something that happened back then."

Seth looked at the book dubiously. "So... You want me to call a bunch of people I haven't talked to since we graduated.

Am I actually supposed to find any information, or just bleat like the goat tied to a stake so you can catch the lion?"

"Oh." She hadn't considered that angle. Maybe enlisting Seth's help was a bad idea. She reached forward to take the yearbook back, but Seth pulled it out of her reach.

"Mom, I'm kidding." He opened the cover and looked at the notes in a myriad of colors and handwriting styles crowded onto the endpaper. "Who was Dylan? I don't remember anyone with that name." Then he flipped to a page in the middle and laughed. "Oh, god, did we really wear stuff like this? And that *hair*!" Charlotte pointed a pudgy finger at a picture. "Yes, she's very silly looking, isn't she?"

From where she sat, Penelope could see no more than a crowd-shaped blur, but she could almost smell the Axe body spray wafting off the pictures. Seth kept turning pages, laughing and cringing in turn.

Leaving her son to his exploration, Penelope looked at Jake. "You still have your high school yearbooks in the garage, don't you?"

He nodded. "The soap was drying on top of that box, so they must be permanently lavender scented by now. Probably have to burn them."

Penelope's soap hadn't technically been a success, with its bubbles and orange-pink color — to say nothing of the dried lavender flowers that were supposed to be pressed on the outside. With her usual failure to follow directions, she'd mixed the flowers in along with everything else, and they had darkened into small pellets that strongly resembled rat turds. The added fragrance had permeated the garage for months as the soap cured. But learning to make horrible soap had helped her catch a murderer, so Penelope remembered the experience fondly.

"You're not allowed to burn them until I look at them. I might need blackmail material after you leave me for some nurse in the retirement home." She wondered what Jake had looked like as a teenager. Knowing him, he'd probably been gorgeous even when Penelope had been trying out awkward hair styles and figuring out who her friends were. Luckily, all evidence of her own high school years had been lost during a move long ago.

He gave her a lazy smile. "I trust you to figure out how to spend it all before it gets to that point."

She returned the smile, then climbed to her feet. "I have to go take care of some pets. Call me if there's any news about Lenz."

CHAPTER 26

*P*iglet and Eeyore greeted Penelope at the door with their normal snuffles of hello. The two fawn pugs usually spent their days with Gary at his machine shop, greeting vendors and customers or snoring on their beds in the corner. This change in the routine, caused by an unplanned trip as Gary's father entered hospice, wasn't to their liking, so Penelope had taken to dropping by three or four times per day instead of the two that Gary was paying her for.

Gary and Jake were friends — the type of friendship Penelope had only seen between men of a certain age, who often drank a cup of coffee at the same diner and never seemed to talk to each other — so Jake had also been coming by. From the random appearance of newspapers and other notes on the counter, as well as perfectly new dog toys and a plush velvet dog bed, at least one other person stopped by to see the dogs regularly. Since half the town went by the machine shop to see the pugs, this didn't surprise Penelope.

Gary had mentioned that other people had the key to his house, so she wouldn't worry if things had moved around, but insisted he would feel better leaving a professional in charge of the dogs' care instead of relying on his friends. "They're a great bunch, but they're not exactly reliable. I've seen what happens when they have to show up at the shop to sign for a delivery," he said, with a lack of judgment Penelope found refreshing. "I'll feel better if I don't have to worry that everyone went to Cancun for the weekend."

Even with all the attention the pugs were getting, they still made a show of pretending they were famished and would wither away if she didn't immediately feed them. Penelope eyed the rapidly dropping level in the treat jar on the counter and adjusted the amount of kibble accordingly. If Gary came back to pugs that looked like blimps on four legs, it wouldn't be Penelope's doing.

Her phone rang as she scooped poop in the backyard, and she continued her grid search as she answered.

"Everything's fine," Seth greeted her. "Jake went to the hospital. He's hoping Lenz might be awake. Or," he added, dropping his voice, "he just didn't want to be here when Hannah woke up and we had to tell her Dad got arrested again."

Another lump went into the bag. "Nah, Jake's made of sterner stuff. How did she take it?"

"Just kind of blinked." Seth's voice crept higher at the end, making it almost a question. "Is that good or bad?"

Penelope considered how to explain it in a way that would make sense to her son. "I think there might not be enough space on the hard drive holding her list of problems to add another one."

With a snort of laughter to tell her she hadn't quite bridged the technology divide, Seth continued. "I just wanted to let you know I finished looking through the yearbook. The only pictures of Ashley I could find are when she was hanging out with David. Maybe I should call him to see who else she would have spent time with..."

Penelope stopped scanning the ground and stood up to stretch her back. "Didn't Emma and David leave town for their honeymoon yesterday?" David's name kept coming up every time anyone talked about Ashley, which made sense, as they were cousins. With any luck, he would have a solid alibi for this attack on Lenz.

"I think they leave tomorrow." Seth paused. "Wait, you don't really believe that *David* would have anything to do with this. David wouldn't hurt a fly."

Penelope went back to scanning the ground. "Well, somebody did. And David was at the wedding, so he could have piloted the drone that picked up the blackmail money."

"Yeah, but all of that applies to *me* as well. And I was in the area when Ashley was killed. Plus, I could have made a copy of Dad's car keys at some point in the last few years."

Penelope shook her head as she pushed bottlebrush branches out of the way so she could peer under them. "I'll add you to the top of the list, if you really want me to. But that still doesn't alter the fact that David and Ashley grew up together. If she was killed to keep her from dragging up something about the past at the wedding..."

The more she thought about it, the worse it seemed. Who would be more likely to keep in touch while she lived in New York than a relative? Who better than David to ensure that Ashley came to town? He had to have known Emma's mother would jump at the chance to include a famous author as part of the wedding. If Ashley had been about to expose something in David's past, how better to ensure she came close enough to be killed?

"Fine," Seth said, clearly agreeing just so they could stop arguing. "But I'll need a lot more proof before I ever believe David had anything to do with it. He's a *pediatrician*."

Seth's logic made her smile. "I doubt he did it either, but is there any way to find out if he has ties to Lone Pine College?"

"He didn't say anything when I asked about Ashley and Lone Pine. I'm pretty sure David did his undergrad at Stanford. But just to prove it wasn't him, I'll ask some people."

"Thank you. Anything else strike you from the yearbook?"

"No, but I'll look through it again. Maybe I'll talk to Mr. Leonard."

"Good idea." Penelope doubted the nerdy science teacher noticed his students' social lives unless they were dressed up as Klingons at the time, but Ethan Leonard always asked after Seth when she ran into him at the grocery store, so she knew he'd appreciate a visit. "Tell him I said hello."

"I will. Are there any plans for dinner?"

"Wedding food, unless you want to organize something else." Piglet bounded over with a crumpled leaf hanging from his mouth.

"Sounds good. Talk to you soon."

After Penelope hung up, the leaf in Piglet's mouth moved, and she realized it was a small brown lizard. "How did you manage to catch...?" She put down her scooping supplies and freed the lizard from the pug's mouth. To her untrained eye, it looked undamaged. She held it near a fence post and was relieved to see it scuttle away.

She frowned at Piglet. "Pugs aren't supposed to hunt. You're supposed to..." She stopped, unable to remember what pugs had been bred for. Whatever it was, that smashed face and chubby body couldn't have been meant for hunting and killing. "You're supposed to be a good boy."

At that last bit, Piglet's curly tail wagged faster and his mouth opened in a canine smile. Penelope scratched his favorite spot and then stood. "Must be time to go for a walk."

Maybe something would come to her.

* * *

No solution to solving the problem of who had murdered two people and injured a third occurred to her while Penelope walked Piglet and Eeyore. She *really* hoped David hadn't been involved — he and Emma seemed like such a good couple.

The answer also eluded her as she chopped vegetables for Jimmy the scarlet macaw and scooped the litter boxes used by Captain Jack and Spiderman. The cats and bird lived together in the same house, with the cats making a wide berth around the huge wrought iron cage in the living room where Jimmy ruled.

Penelope was sweeping the floor when Captain Jack walked past, yowling around the stuffed mouse held in his mouth.

From the living room came, "Shut up! Shut up! Shut up!" The voice was male, with a strong New York accent. Since their owner, Cherise, was female and had grown up in Seattle, Penelope had always assumed the macaw was mimicking a former owner, and she had a pretty good idea why Jimmy had been re-homed.

Since Jimmy yelling "Shut up!" often led to Jimmy rattling off a string of expletives loud enough to be heard a block away, Penelope intervened. She yelled, "Cowabunga!"

"Cowabunga!" Jimmy's approximation of the Teenage Mutant Ninja Turtles was far closer than hers had been. "Cowabunga!" Then his voice changed. "I hate it when he does that."

Now that she'd switched Jimmy over to quoting TMNT, Penelope turned her attention back to Captain Jack. "Where's your brother?"

Spiderman had gained his name when he'd been brought home as a kitten and promptly disappeared for two days.

Cherise had finally found him behind a fake plant in the display nook above the front door, easily ten feet off the ground. He still hid when strangers came over, though Cherise said he sat on her lap when she settled on the couch.

The first time Penelope had taken care of Cherise's pets, she'd spent forty-five minutes searching through the house for Spiderman. Then she'd learned that Captain Jack would lead her straight to him. "Where's your brother?" she asked again.

Captain Jack dropped the bedraggled mouse toy and trotted up the stairs. In this house, the living room had vaulted ceilings that reached to the second floor, so Jimmy watched her climbing the stairs. "The enemy of my enemy is my bro!"

"Cowabunga!" Penelope replied, putting extra energy in her voice. Jimmy, like most parrots, responded to excitement — which probably explained his extensive repertoire of curses and commands.

Captain Jack dove under the bed in the master bedroom, and Spiderman ran out. They tussled while Penelope watched from the doorway.

"Okay, just needed to make sure he was in the house and doing well." Penelope went back down the stairs, leaving the two cats rolling around on the floor behind her. "Your mom is back tomorrow morning." In the kitchen, she wrote a note for Cherise, letting her know how everyone had fared.

Through the open window, she heard the doorbell from the next house ring.

From the living room, a voice called, "Hello?"

It was such a good imitation of Cherise's voice, Penelope thought for a moment the other woman had come home a day early. But she peeked around the corner just in time to see Jimmy say, "Just a minute! I'll be right there!"

Penelope wondered how long people waited on Cherise's porch for her to answer the door when she wasn't home.

"Hello? Hello? Just a minute! I'll be right there!"

The tone really was perfect, just as if Cherise were standing right in the living room. Penelope realized she needed to talk to her husband about alibis.

CHAPTER 27

*J*ake was on a ladder cleaning the gutters at Esther's house when Penelope arrived. Ostensibly, Penelope was there to scoop the litter boxes, a task Esther found difficult with her arthritis. In reality, the cats would have been fine for another day, but Penelope always enjoyed talking to her friend.

She stood on the sidewalk watching Jake scoop leaves into a bag, his entire body strong, balanced, and graceful. Once he began climbing down the ladder, she did her best imitation of a wolf whistle. "Hey, baby, you available to rent for other jobs?"

"Only if my wife doesn't find out," he called back without looking at her. Then he turned around and did an exaggerated double-take. "Oh, it's *you*."

They grinned at each other as Penelope skipped up the walkway. She leaned into him for a kiss, appreciating that he kept his gloves covered with slimy leaves away from her. "How is Lenz doing?"

"Made it through surgery. As long as there aren't any complications, he should make a full recovery."

"Good. Are you done out here? I had a thought."

"Just one last section. I'll be inside in a few minutes." He turned, picked up the ladder, and leaned it against the house six feet away.

Penelope watched him climb the ladder, torn between admiring his figure and worrying that he might hurt himself. But since she wasn't actually keeping him from harm by standing on Esther's lawn, and he might be safer if she wasn't around to distract him, she climbed the ramp to Esther's front door.

At her knock, Esther called, "It's open!" Penelope slipped inside, ready to block the white cat who had lately decided he wanted to run outside, but the cats were busy rolling in catnip on the hardwood floor in the living room. The house smelled of chicken broth and onions. She found Esther in the kitchen, removing bones from a pot of stock. "Oh good, you're here. I was running out of tasks for that young man of yours, and he doesn't like to sit still."

Penelope smiled at the appellation and the truth. "Not without a golf tournament on television." She went back down the hall to the room with the litter boxes, raising her voice to compensate for the distance. "You heard about Lenz being run over?"

"Yes, and Todd's car being used." The clang of a lid being set on the pot followed her words, then the quiet whirr of the motorized wheelchair. "Your ex-husband may be a lot of things, but I don't believe he'd murder anyone in cold blood." By the time Esther had finished speaking, she was at the doorway.

Penelope raked through the sand. "If you'd asked me a month ago which one of us would be sitting in jail today, I would have bet Jake's entire pension it would be me, not Todd."

"You would have found it hard to find someone to bet against you."

"Right?" Penelope paused, imagining it. "If I'd known, I could have made a fortune. We could have..." That part stumped her. She already had everything she needed, and the common dream of lying around on a tropical beach while servants brought her drinks made her skin itch. "I don't know. We could have stuffed a mattress with cash or something."

There was a pause as they both thought that over. Then Esther sighed. "That sounds like a recipe for insomnia."

Penelope nodded and moved to the next litter box. "But maybe I'd finally get Jake to go mattress shopping with me." Every time she brought up the idea of replacing their increasingly lumpy mattress, Jake suddenly found urgent business elsewhere.

"You think so?"

"Probably not." Penelope finished scooping and grabbed the broom to sweep up the litter the cats tracked out of the boxes. "They always say money doesn't buy happiness. Maybe that's why." She held the broom out of the way as the calico covered in bits of dried catnip dashed into the room, pushed off the wall, and sprinted out again. "Though I notice the people saying that aren't poor."

"Money may not buy happiness, but lack of it can make you miserable." Esther reversed her chair so Penelope could get past with the trash bag. "Speaking of people with too much money, I ran into Joann at the Rose Garden Society plant sale this morning."

"Really?" Penelope tried not to laugh as she briefly ducked outside to put the bag in the wheeled bin. "For some reason, I figured she would just go off to Hawaii for a few months until she thought everyone had forgotten about the wedding."

"Everyone else did, too. But she showed up to run the hosta table just as she always does. Looked about twenty years older, but that might have been because she didn't have a dab of makeup on."

Facing away from Esther as she washed her hands, Penelope grimaced. "I refuse to feel sorry for her. She brought that entire thing on herself."

"Yes. I can't decide if she's truly affected or if this is just another attempt at manipulation. Only time will tell."

"What will time tell?" Jake entered the kitchen and moved to the sink next to Penelope to use the faucet after she had finished rinsing her hands.

"If Joann learned a lesson from what happened with the wedding." She handed him the towel. "I'm not holding my breath."

"Probably a good idea." He inhaled deeply. "Smells good in here."

Esther had started ladling chicken stock into plastic containers. "Come over for lunch tomorrow and we'll have noodle soup. I'll bake some rolls."

Jake nodded. "Assuming I'm not at the courthouse." He frowned and looked at Penelope. "The judge may not give Todd bail this time."

"Can you blame them? Two hours after he gets out, it looks like he tried to kill yet another person." She gritted her teeth. "It feels so unfair that I can't just gloat about him being in jail and I have to actually *help* him."

Jake wrapped one arm around her waist and kissed her temple. "I'm sure this suffering will make you a better person."

"Maybe I don't want to *be* a better person. Have you ever thought of that? Maybe I'm already good enough the way I am."

Jake's face became suspiciously innocent as he turned to Esther. "Lunch tomorrow would be wonderful."

Penelope elbowed him even as she laughed. Then she frowned. "What was...?" There was something she had meant to ask Esther about. "Oh, I remember now. Of the kids around Ashley's age, did any of them have ties to Lone Pine College?" Esther had taught kindergarten, so she didn't always know much about her pupils after they left the primary grades and went to a different school. But then again, Esther knew everyone in town, and she held a major role in the active social network.

"Lone Pine College? Let me think." She retrieved the pitcher of lemonade from the refrigerator and moved to the table.

Penelope and Jake grabbed three tumblers and followed, seating themselves in the battered wooden chairs.

"If you had asked that about students twenty years earlier, it would have been a long list. Lone Pine is fairly small, and while it *used* to have a good reputation as a liberal arts college, there was a scandal about twenty years ago — grades for cash, if I remember correctly — and it never quite recovered. Ever since then, we haven't sent many students there." Esther poured lemonade into the three tumblers as she spoke. "For young people who want to really get away from their parents, it's too close to home. And for those staying in the area, there are better choices; the state university is more prestigious, and Hopper-Redding has a far better program, for those looking for a smaller school."

Penelope gave Jake a doubtful look. "Maybe Edie's sabotaged car isn't related after all."

"Hold on, don't be so hasty." Esther leveled her best sit-down-so-we-can-have-story-time look at Penelope, and Penelope folded her hands in her lap. "Just because we don't send many doesn't mean the number is zero. Dawn Lysak would have been a year or two ahead of Ashley, but they likely had friends in common. And Joy Callealt, though she was a good four years after Ashley, so maybe less likely. There was talk of Sean Salinger going there; his parents moved during his senior year, and I'm not sure where he ended up. Billy Doyle... No, he would have been too young for your group."

Jake wrote the names on the pad of paper he carried around. "This gives us a start."

"You might have better luck driving up there. They keep a photo of each graduating class in the main hall, and there's a list of names." Esther leaned back as the wide-eyed calico jumped on her lap and immediately raced away. She picked up her lemonade as if nothing had happened. "They all enjoy a bit of catnip, but I sometimes forget how wild Timmie gets."

Penelope looked at Jake's orderly handwriting. "Is there anything else out there? We know the victim taught at the college, and she had a history of relationships with students, but if she just had cougar tendencies, it could have been someone from another college in the area. Or someone who lived nearby."

Next to her, Jake wrote "cougar tendencies" in the margin and put a box around the words.

"There's not really much else out there." Esther thought about that as she sipped her lemonade. "Except during the summer, of course."

Many of the smaller towns in the state had a summer festival to help boost tourism revenue. And because tourists were occasionally whimsical people, for the past thirty years there had been a lively competition for a town brand that would attract the curious without bringing the true believers — the former having money to spend and the latter having the reputation of using more resources than they brought with them.

Historical themes were safe, but unlikely to overfill the coffers. A celebration of the most common locally grown vegetable worked, as long as it was harvested at a convenient time. For a small town, local legends were usually the best choice; they required a bit more advertising, but that brought tourists during the rest of the year as well.

"Let me guess. The Gold Miner and his Nine Wives Festival?"

Esther laughed. "No, their summer festival is Donkey Days. Donkey rides for the kids, costume contests, cookies shaped like donkeys, chocolate shaped like donkey droppings, that sort of thing."

Even knowing it was a blatant money grab, Penelope was tempted. When she looked at Jake's notepad, he had just finished writing "Donkey Days?"

But Esther waved that away. "That might bring someone for a few hours, but if you're looking for people staying in the area long enough for a relationship, the leadership course is a better bet."

Penelope met Jake's eyes, and he shook his head. This leadership course wasn't something he knew about either.

Esther explained. "The Lang Foundation runs a course on the Lone Pine campus during the summer when most of the college students are gone. Two months of classes and leadership exercises. It has a reputation for making resumes attractive, especially for things like getting into medical school. And to be fair, most of the course graduates have done very well." She gave them a wry look. "But it's generally attended by young people who can afford not to work during the summer and also afford the foundation's course fee."

Penelope nodded in understanding. Students from a wealthy background, Esther meant. With access to tutors and better schools and family connections, they were already at an advantage. Those people were probably going to do well no matter what training they had. "I wonder if there's a list of alumni somewhere." Even knowing her wishes were ridiculous, Penelope hoped David's name wasn't there.

Jake flipped his notebook closed. "I'm sure it will be online. Groups like that depend on being able to point to successful attendees so they can charge whatever they want." He turned his head to look at Penelope. "What's wrong?"

She sighed. "Seth told me that Ashley and David are in a lot of the yearbook pictures together. And David's a pediatrician. He would have been looking for an edge on his med school applications."

Esther gave a small shake of her head. "Surely David would have been too busy with the wedding all weekend..."

"That's the thing. We know the wedding party wasn't together when Ashley was murdered. Emma and her maid of honor were scrambling to fix the table arrangements, but in Joann's mind, the role of the groom is to show up on time and say 'I do', so he had free time." Penelope took a deep breath and let it out slowly so she didn't give an impassioned rant on gender expectations in the wedding industry. Jake patted her knee. "Kieran was in a meeting on his computer..."

That reminded her of Jimmy yelling *Hello?* in Cherise's voice and her earlier thought. "Is there any way to fake a meeting? Or not a meeting, but attendance at a meeting — could you do some sort of thing where a fake computer person could make it look like you're at the meeting?"

They all exchanged uncertain looks. Jake said, "I know you can change the *background* in a virtual meeting, but I don't see how you could show a person who wasn't there."

Esther nodded. "And wouldn't he need to speak at some point? Even if the computer could mimic his voice, it would still need to know what to say and when to say it."

Penelope sagged in her seat. It had all seemed so obvious when she was listening to the parrot answering the neighbor's doorbell. "I guess I should be glad the computers can't fool everyone so easily."

"Give it a few years." Jake finished his lemonade and got up to put their glasses in the dishwasher. "In the meantime, let's look up who's attended those leadership courses."

CHAPTER 28

inner that evening was a chaotic affair, with a smattering of wedding food plus macaroni and cheese. Charlotte's original dinner of chicken nuggets in the shape of dinosaurs had been snatched from the high chair by Brutus while Penelope was cleaning ketchup from Frodo's ears. As Hannah had said, they could handle the dogs or the toddler, but when they all ganged up, there was no stopping them.

By the time everyone had eaten, and Charlotte had finished her bath and then had a series of books read to her, Penelope was ready to go to bed as well. She hadn't had this many people staying in the house since... Never. Twice, Jake's friend Brian had visited for a few days, and Seth had spent a few weekends, but they'd never had a full house for this long.

She sat on the couch, back against Jake's shoulder and computer in her lap, and listened as Hannah read Charlotte's favorite book for the third time. Seth was baking cookies in the kitchen with both dogs in close attendance. All in all, the house felt cozy, despite the reason for their extra guests.

"Hey, Mom? Is this regular flour?" Seth stood in the

doorway to the kitchen, holding the unlabeled container. "It looks a little funny."

It looked like that because Penelope had mixed in the last bit of whole wheat flour, figuring it wouldn't really matter for the things she baked. "Mostly all-purpose flour. It should be fine for cookies."

Penelope's baking supplies languished because, more often than not, the results were a disaster. Unlike cooking, which encouraged experimentation, baking required precise measurements and following directions, two of Penelope's weakest points. After her most recent attempt at sourdough bread had left even Brutus unsure about eating it, she'd decided store-bought was fine. Even the cheapest brand always tasted better than her best homemade loaf. Jake had supportively eaten everything she'd given him, but she noticed that after she'd given up, the loaf pans had migrated to the very back of the cupboard over the refrigerator, a spot she couldn't reach without getting out the step stool.

Seth blinked, shook his head, and returned to the kitchen.

The Lang Foundation leadership course attendees weren't hard to find, though she did have to scroll past individual biographies of the most influential graduates to get to each year's photo. As expected, the students had been overwhelmingly male and white, with a smugness Penelope associated with money. The most recent year had one Black woman, listed as the recipient of the Ford Opportunity Scholarship — her eyes had a fire lacking in the men around her; Penelope suspected she would outshine the rest in a few years.

As she'd feared, David's smiling face was in the first row of the group picture from the year Speedy Edie had died. "Dang it. I was hoping to be wrong about that." If David had been staying in Lone Pine that summer, he could have been the one who sent Edie's car off the road.

"Not so fast." Jake leaned over and zoomed in on the figures at the side. "Look who else was there."

Lenz's cowlick stood up despite what looked like large quantities of gel meant to hold it down. His face seemed softer, not quite the visage of a man who could ask people questions about a tragedy with an unwavering gaze.

And at the edge of the picture, looking to the side as if something had distracted him, was Kieran.

"Lenz *and* Kieran were there. I guess I shouldn't be so surprised. Boys that age run around in a pack, and all three of them were hoping to go on to bigger and better things after college." Penelope scrolled up to see all the biographies she'd sped past, and there they were: David's residency and fellowship, Lenz's advanced journalism degree and on-camera work, and Kieran's rising political star.

Jake tapped the arrow key to scroll down. "I think we can safely remove Lenz from the running."

Penelope nodded and closed her laptop. "He could have paid someone to pretend to run him down in Todd's car, but it almost killed him. That's taking an alibi too far."

Taking the laptop from her, Jake set it down on a crumb-free spot of the coffee table. "Not to say I haven't seen stupider attempts to create an alibi, but I think Lenz would be a lot more careful about anything that might leave scars on his face."

"Hey, Mom? Do you have anything other than these baby eggs?" Seth stood by the side of the couch holding two speckled quail eggs.

"No, but those should be fine for baking. Use as many as you can."

Jake stirred. "You'll want to use three for every one egg the recipe calls for."

Seth nodded doubtfully as he looked at the eggs. "Where did you get these?"

"A friend of ours started keeping quail." Rosa had under-estimated the number of eggs thirty quail would produce; Penelope bought a container as often as she could until Rosa built up her customer base.

Jake had laughed about making a ten-egg omelet for the two of them, but he'd gone to refill their supply the last time and come back an hour later with the contented smile of a man who has been listening to the gentle chirps of quail; he'd even talked about building a quail hutch for them. Then Brutus had barreled around the corner, knocked into Jake, careened into his water dish, and run back out. In the resulting silence, broken only by the water dripping from the walls, Jake had sighed and given up on keeping quail.

Seth went back to the kitchen, juggling the eggs as he walked. He was out of sight when Penelope heard something hit the floor, followed by scrabbling dog feet. "Oops."

A raw egg wasn't the worst thing Brutus and Frodo had ever eaten, possibly not even in the previous twenty-four hours. Penelope settled in closer against Jake's shoulder. "He would have figured out how many to use."

"I've been living with you for too long. If someone told you to use as many as you could, you would see it as a chal-lenge and invent the cookie frittata." After a few seconds of silence, he turned his head to look at her. "No. Don't do it. There are some things that aren't meant to be."

"I was just thinking..."

Hannah emerged from the guest bedroom, carefully closing the door behind her. "I think she's down for the count, but I've been wrong before." She sank into the armchair. "I can't thank you enough for letting us stay here."

"We're happy to have you," Penelope responded automati-cally. And it was true, if for no other reason than helping Hannah and Charlotte made Seth feel better. "You don't know of any bad blood between Todd and David, do you? Or

Todd and Kieran?" Maybe there was a reason Todd had been set up beyond being a convenient target.

"The best man and the groom? I don't think Todd had met either of them before he drove down here for the wedding. Todd and Emma know each other well enough to talk to at family reunions and that sort of thing, but they aren't particularly close."

Penelope sighed. "There goes that theory. I think Todd was just in the wrong place at the wrong time." Granted, if he hadn't been a jerk, he wouldn't have been there at all, but Hannah didn't need to be reminded of that.

"I think..." Hannah paused, then sat up straighter and started again. "I'm going to start a business online running social media campaigns. That's what I did at my old job before I had Charlotte, and I was good at it. But with the expense of daycare and Todd traveling so much, we decided it made sense for me to stay home full time." She rubbed her belly absently. "Now... I think it would be good for me to have my own job, even if it doesn't earn much for a while. If I run my own business online, I can choose my hours and I won't have to commute."

Penelope understood it wasn't as much of a conversational swerve as it had initially sounded. Clearly, Hannah understood Todd's peripheral involvement in the initial murder could have been avoided, and now she was thinking of the needs of herself and her children. "I think that's a great idea. It's been a while since I did all the paperwork to get my business license, but let me know if you have any questions." She turned her head. "Or ask Jake. He filed everything for the investigation business just a little while ago, so he probably remembers it."

Jake nodded.

"And Seth could set up your website if you need help with

that." Penelope had no qualms about offering her son's technical services.

As if she'd called him, Seth appeared. "What am I helping with?"

"Hannah's going to start an online business running social media campaigns."

Seth nodded at Hannah. "Good idea. You used to do that before you had Charlotte, didn't you? Remind me later — I have a friend who might be looking for someone in a few months." He turned to Penelope and held up the electric mixer in one hand and a single beater in the other. "Do you know where the other beater is? It's not in the box."

Penelope winced. "Sorry. Brutus mangled it and I keep forgetting to order a new set." In hindsight, offering to let Brutus lick the beater had been a bad idea. He'd grabbed it from her and gnawed on it before she could get it away from him. While he hadn't swallowed anything, the metal had been bent beyond repair.

"That explains why Brutus got so excited when I took it out of the cupboard. I guess I'm mixing everything by hand."

Penelope levered herself off the couch and followed him into the kitchen, where a tidy array of measured ingredients took up most of the free space on the counter. "Brave of you to leave the room with butter out in the open."

Seth packed the mixer back in its box. "Brutus and I have come to an understanding. He behaves, and I give him a treat every now and then."

Penelope raised one eyebrow and looked at the mastiff. Once again, Frodo had claimed the middle of the dog bed, so Brutus spilled over onto the floor. He had his front legs crossed and appeared to be the picture of innocence. Usually, that meant he had just gotten into something he wasn't supposed to. "Right."

"You guys let him get away with too much, Mom. He knows you're a pushover, so he takes advantage."

"Uh huh." She cast her eye over the contents on the counter. "You might want to make sure there are enough eggs left before you get started here."

"I already..." Seth picked up the bowl where two tiny quail eggs remained, then set it down and cast a disappointed look at the mastiff. "Buddy, we had an agreement." He focused on Frodo. "And *you* were supposed to let me know if he was getting into trouble."

Brutus wagged his tail. Frodo sat on his hind legs with his front legs held together in the air.

Seth shook his head. "No way. I'm not giving you guys a treat for that... Okay, fine, but just one, and you have to promise to be better next time."

"Truly, your dog training skills are a wonder to behold."

Seth grinned as he got more eggs out of the refrigerator. "Pretty bad, huh? It's probably good I have a different job that pays the bills."

"To be fair, I'm not sure it's even possible to train Brutus to leave food untouched. The best you can do is reduce temptation." She watched her son carefully break six tiny eggs into a bowl. "I have a computer question for you."

Seth didn't pause in cracking the next egg. "Save everything and reboot. You know that fixes almost everything."

Considering the number of times she'd called him for help and that had been the solution, Penelope decided she deserved that; she let it slide. "Different kind of computer question. If someone is in a remote meeting, can they make it look like they're in one place while they're really in another?"

"Sure." He used a fork to whisk the eggs together. "Almost all meeting software has an option to replace your background with something else. If it looks like you're sitting on a beach, nobody has to know how many energy drink cans are piled up on the desk. The edges blur if you move too fast, though. I don't think you could really fool anyone."

"How about the person, though — can you make it look like you're sitting there when you're off doing something else?"

Seth glanced over before he looked at the recipe. "I take it this is about Kieran's alibi during the time Ashley was murdered?" He added the butter and sugar to a large bowl and stirred. After a few turns, he adjusted his grip on the bowl and stabbed at a chunk of butter with the spoon. "At least now I know what to get you for your birthday." The scent of butter and brown sugar wafted across the kitchen as he stirred. "It depends on how involved he was in the meeting."

Penelope's pulse quickened. It sounded like he was saying it might be possible. "What do you mean by involved?"

"Well..." Seth added a quarter of the dry ingredients and went back to stirring. "As a purely hypothetical case, if your boss's boss sets up a mandatory meeting with a hundred employees to explain the new vision for the group and you have better things to do, you *could* record a one minute video of yourself and then have the meeting software play that in a loop while you go out to lunch."

Penelope ignored the confession underlying his words. If Seth's boss's boss wanted everyone to pay attention, he should have made the meeting more interesting or not made it mandatory. "And nobody would notice?"

"Not unless someone asks a question. It wouldn't work in one of our small design meetings where we're constantly going back and forth. But for a big meeting with one person talking? It works perfectly."

"But you'd be able to tell if you went back over the recording, right? I mean, if you had reason to suspect someone had done that."

"With a recording? Absolutely. Nobody sits completely still for an hour, and whatever movements you make in your looped recording are going to be repeated every minute." Seth dumped more of the dry ingredients in the bowl and flexed his fingers before taking up the spoon and stirring again. "It all sort of depends on nobody really caring enough to call you out."

Penelope sank back into the chair. "It sounds like something they would have noticed." The police would have been looking for that sort of thing when they examined the recording. At least, they should have been. "Would you be willing to look at the recording anyhow? You might see something everyone else missed."

"Send me the link. I'll look at it before I go to bed."

As Seth often didn't turn out his light until the early hours of the morning, Penelope resigned herself to the delay. "Thank you."

"No problem." Seth surveyed the contents of the bowl. "You don't have any dried fruit or anything, do you? Other than those apricots."

"What happened to the apricots?" When Seth gave a furtive glance toward Brutus, she shook her head. "He didn't eat the plastic bag, did he?"

"No. I had them on the cutting board and turned my back for just a second..."

"That's why I usually lock him in the yard while I'm cooking." She turned her thoughts back to what was in the refrigerator. "We have some frozen figs. Would that do?"

Seth shrugged. "Sure. Why not?"

Penelope smiled at this evidence that her son had ended up with some of her traits. If Todd had ever baked cookies and found one ingredient lacking, he would have placed everything on hold and gone to the grocery store.

Opening the freezer door brought a burst of activity from

the dogs. Penelope cleared her throat and waited until they went back to the bed again. She handed the figs to Seth and then gave the dogs a treat. "Dang it, I forgot to call animal services today."

"About Frodo?"

At the sound of his name, the little dog looked up.

"Well, technically, they're supposed to have custody of him. I think. They should at least know he's here."

"Right."

"We don't mind fostering him, but it's not a permanent arrangement."

"Of course not."

"It's *not*." Penelope swiped a spoonful of batter. Sugar, butter, and... almond? "Did you intend to use almond extract instead of vanilla? Frodo's just here until they track down Ashley's mother."

"Of course he is." Seth picked up the almond extract bottle, read the label, and shrugged before dumping the chopped figs into the bowl. "He looks awfully comfortable sharing that bed with Brutus, though."

Penelope shook her head and walked out of the kitchen. "I'll send you that link."

CHAPTER 29

*T*he next morning, Penelope checked her email while sitting on the rectory kitchen floor with Spot's head in her lap. Jake had stayed behind to make pancakes for a wide-awake Charlotte while the rest of the house slept. Spot kept eyeing Jake's usual position on the floor and sighing, as if this break in routine troubled her.

"I don't know how people work on these things." Penelope held her phone out, concentrating on the tiny text. "If you make the font big enough to see, you have to scroll three times just to get to the end of the sentence."

Spot wagged her tail in sympathy.

Amid the usual spam and pleas for campaign donations was a message from Seth sent at two in the morning. *Found this. Thought you might find it interesting.* And then there was a link.

Penelope had learned to skip anything with links if the text didn't say exactly what it was for, having once downloaded a virus that way. Dealing with the people at the computer store had been worse than just leaving the virus in place. But this was exactly the sort of message Seth would send if he had noticed something in the recording of Kieran's meeting. "Why he couldn't just tell me what he found, I'll never know."

Spot shifted her position in a way that made it clear that she would never be so unreasonable.

Penelope clicked on the link. Instead of a remote meeting, a video game took over her screen. Or no, not the game, but a recording of someone else playing the game. Three muscled wolf-men bounded across the terrain, attacking demons with swords as they fought their way to a tower in the distance. Above the sounds of carnage and music, three men talked to each other in excited tones, with a mix of laughter and yelling she recognized from years of watching her son play. Had Seth accidentally sent her mail intended for someone else? He'd been pretty careful about that sort of thing after she'd made him explain all the abbreviations he'd used in one misdirected message.

Then she noticed the timestamp ticking along in the corner. Adjusting for time zones... this game had been played right around the time Ashley was killed. Seth had told her players recorded games, and successful runs were often viewed by thousands of people. So maybe Seth *had* meant to send this. On-screen, the three wolf-men crashed through the tower door and fought their way up stone steps. Spot watched the screen, ears pricked.

Zooming in on the names until they were big enough to read didn't help at all. Presumably "Sherlockian", "ZebraCarnage", and "JokerDaddy" meant something — they didn't help her identify the players.

But one voice sounded familiar.

The wolf-men reached a landing where one opened a treasure chest. Another protested. "If we're going to take down Bonser, we need to keep going. I have to leave for the rehearsal dinner in fifteen minutes."

An argument over leaving weapons behind was cut short by one character running up the next flight of stairs. The other two followed, but Penelope wasn't paying attention anymore. She rubbed Spot's shoulder absently as the wolf-men made it to the top of the tower and battled the evil wizard.

David had an alibi.

* * *

SQUIRRELS CHITTERED in the trees as Penelope and Jake jogged by with Heidi. The pace was slow enough to carry on a conversation, letting Penelope work through her thoughts. "Somehow we had all these suspects and we've proved it wasn't any of them. Except for Todd, who is one of the few I'm *sure* didn't do it."

As expected, the arraignment that morning had gone poorly, with the judge refusing to release Todd on bail for the new charges, opining that he appeared to be a danger to the community.

Jake ducked under a wayward branch. "Which means we either missed someone from the start, or the killer manufactured a plausible alibi."

"Ugh. We need to go over everything again, don't we? That's so much like *work*."

Jake glanced over, a grin on his face, but he didn't point out that it really was work, and some people had full-time jobs with benefits for doing just that. Penelope noted he'd also stopped suggesting they leave it all to the police.

"There's another thing that's bugging me," she said as they continued. "How long does it take to write a book?"

"The longest thing I've ever written was an essay comparing and contrasting *Pride and Prejudice* to *Beowulf*. Forty-three pages in one weekend."

Penelope shot him a look of disbelief.

Jake coughed. "I quoted from the source material heavily. Since I hadn't actually read either book, I was going for quantity over quality."

"Did it work?"

"I passed." He shrugged. "But we probably shouldn't extrapolate from that. Why do you ask?"

"*One Wild Night* came out a year after Edie died. But is that enough time? Ashley would have had to write the novel, and find an agent, and all the other stuff that happens before a book ends up in stores." Penelope was fuzzy about the steps, but she'd seen an interview with a famous author who claimed he'd forgotten what his book was about by the time it was finally released. "It just seems like the timeline might be off."

"Ah."

"No opinion?"

"I don't know enough about it. Do you want me to make something up?"

"Please. I'd love to hear from someone who compared two books he hadn't read."

"Okay." Jake drew himself up straighter as he ran. "We should definitely keep that in mind." His stride went back to normal. "Is that good enough?"

"Perfect." Penelope moved behind him to avoid a branch sticking out into the path. "Forty-three pages? Really?"

"It was a strong candidate for the golden shovel award."

They jogged without speaking for half a block, Heidi's tags jingling with every step. At the intersection, Jake gestured to the left. "Through the park?"

Penelope almost agreed automatically, but pointed forward instead. "Yes, but let's make a wider loop to get there. Kevin Nelson spread cow manure over their yard yesterday, and it's pretty stinky."

After checking for traffic, Jake headed across the street. "He's going to kill his plants if he's putting down uncomposted manure."

"He's going to get uninvited from every party and cookout if he isn't careful. You can smell it from a block away. Esther's had a steady stream of people coming to her house to talk about it this morning." Penelope had stopped by to scoop litter boxes and found the neighborhood in the sort of uproar usually only found when someone cut down a beloved tree or started construction on an addition that threw off the proportions of the house.

"Maybe Kevin did it on purpose."

They shared a smile. Loretta Nelson loved getting out and interacting with people. She was in two book clubs and a painting group, and volunteered to teach English learners at the library five days a week. She saw their three grown children and four grandchildren often.

In contrast, her husband wanted to spend his retirement sitting in his living room watching documentaries on World War II, and he expected his wife to be available to do the cooking, laundry, shopping, and cleaning up after him, just as she'd done when he'd worked full-time. His duties began and ended with lawn care. On the rare occasions Kevin went to parties, he sat near the door, glaring at everyone and checking his watch.

"I wonder what it would take to make him wake up." At Jake's worried look, she held up her hands. "I'm not planning anything, just wondering."

"If he hasn't figured it out in seventy years, it's not looking good." Jake shook his head.

"Yes, but Sally and her wife are buying a new house, and it has a separate apartment in the back." Penelope and Heidi moved over to run in the grass while Jake shifted into the street, letting two children on bicycles take over the sidewalk. When the kids had passed, the runners moved back to their former positions.

"And Sally is...?"

"Loretta and Kevin's middle daughter."

"Ah." They turned left at the next block. When they were back on the sidewalk together, Jake continued. "So you think Loretta has an exit plan."

"When she told me about the new house, she mentioned the apartment twice."

"Sounds like a sign." He put a hand on her shoulder to warn her of the car backing out of the driveway in front of them. "Good for her."

"Probably better than hitting him over the head and burying him in the backyard." Penelope considered that. "Though she'd end up in a much better situation financially. And I'm pretty sure the whole neighborhood would help her cover it up."

"Remember, murder is wrong."

"Fine, have it your way. Spoilsport."

"When all this is over, let's go out to dinner." He pulled ahead so they could go single file around a garden tote blocking the path.

Penelope eyed him, taking in his easy stride and the sweat dotting his t-shirt. Going out to dinner, as opposed to picking up takeout, implied dressing up and eating at a nice restaurant, something usually reserved for celebrations. She thought about what would occasion that and hit on the most obvious. "We got paid."

A smile took over his face as he jogged in place, waiting for her to catch up. "Money hit the account this morning."

While searching for the four women from the polaroids hadn't been the first paid job of his fledgling investigative business, it had been the first that hadn't come by way of friends or family. Not that tracking down lost or stolen items for someone in the neighborhood wasn't interesting — but this case had come from a lawyer who'd chosen Jake because, after two expensive failures, he needed an investigator willing to work on a contingency basis.

Knowing Jake, the source of his joy was having a satisfied client who would almost certainly generate more business. Penelope just wanted to crow about their shoestring agency having solved a case that two big organizations had failed on. Not that she would admit it aloud, at least not to anyone other than Jake. And maybe Esther.

They reached the park, eschewing the paved path clogged with strollers in favor of the dirt track that ran alongside. From behind the chain-link fence with its green slats came the buzz of mini-drones on the smaller daytime obstacle course. Heidi watched a hare dash to safety without more than a twitch of her ears, making Penelope snort. If Brutus had been there, he would have barreled through everything to chase after the hare, leaving a swath of destruction behind him.

Jake clearly had similar thoughts. "We could have adopted a dog like Heidi." His voice held equal parts humor and wistfulness.

"There's no *we* on that one. Brutus is all your fault." While Penelope had found the body of Brutus's previous owner, Jake had been the one to agree to the former mayor's request to temporarily board the dog. "Remind me to call animal services today to let them know we have Frodo." She stopped jogging and stared at the fence hiding the golf course.

Jake had only gone three steps before he realized she was no longer with him and turned around. "What's wrong?"

"Why don't the neighbors complain about the drones?"

Jake followed her gaze, then looked back at her. "They aren't that loud."

"Not the noise." She rewound her thoughts. "It's not so much what they do, it's what they *don't* do."

Jake's grin made the laugh lines at the corners of his eyes stand out. "I know you think that's an explanation, but you might need to make another pass at it."

Heidi bumped her nose against Penelope's leg to remind her they were out here to run, not stand and stare. Penelope broke into a jog again. "Okay, pretend you rented drones to a bunch of drunk people. What are the odds they are all going to stick to spots on the golf course and not scout the neighborhood? The rental spot is at the corner of the golf course, so it's not just a distance boundary."

"But one of them did leave the course," Jake pointed out.

"Ignore the one that picked up the blackmail money for a moment. All those drones, all those weddings. How are the neighbors not up in arms? Our block had one drone, and people would have burned down the owner's house if we'd known who was flying it."

Jake's stride hitched. "They have some way to fence off the course."

"I think they must." She frowned. "I should have flown one off the course when I was there."

"You came the closest."

"That wasn't on purpose." Penelope dodged around a gopher hole. "So maybe the blackmail drone didn't come from someone at the wedding?"

Jake altered direction, heading toward the golf course entrance. "Let's go find out."

CHAPTER 30

"*M*a'am? Excuse me, ma'am?" Penelope and Jake had just started up the cement walkway leading toward the mini drone rental shack when a man in a green polo shirt embroidered with the golf club logo burst out of the pro shop. "You can't bring a dog in here."

Penelope touched Jake's arm. "I'll meet you outside." If they were so serious about the rule that an employee had to sprint, she wouldn't be able to talk her way out of it. She understood the rule even if she didn't like it. Heidi was on-leash and perfectly well behaved. But for all they knew, she might have been like Brutus — the mastiff would have destroyed multiple drones, dug a hole in the green, chased a golf ball, and left an odorous trail from everything he'd gotten into in the last two days. After living with Brutus, Penelope understood why so many places didn't allow dogs.

She turned around. Then she recognized the young man running toward her, his red hair flopping with every stride. "Tick?" At some point she must have known his given name, but so many of her son's friends exclusively used nicknames that she'd lost track of which given name went with each child. Tick was the much younger brother of Seth's friend Boom, whose real name Penelope also didn't remember.

"Ms. Standing?" He slowed to a halt well out of range of the six-foot leash, but he had a genuine smile. "Sorry, I didn't recognize you. How have you been?"

"Fine, thank you." She glanced at his shirt, where *Conlan* had been neatly stitched under the logo. "Sorry, you probably use your real name now." It seemed impossible that the child always running after the older boys was now grown enough to be this young man. Taken to its logical conclusion, that would mean she had aged the same number of years, and that didn't seem possible.

"It's okay. Most of my friends still call me Tick." He tilted his head at the pro shop. "But my boss insists on calling me Conlan, so..." He went down on one knee and held out a hand. "Beautiful dog."

"She belongs to a client." Penelope kept the leash loose and urged Heidi forward. The German Shepherd liked new people, and soon she was leaning against Tick as he scratched her chest. "I only wish my own dog was this well behaved."

He looked up with a wide smile. "That's right! You ended up with the mayor's dog, didn't you? How is he?"

"Brutus is doing really well." Brutus had belonged to both Jezza *and* her ex-husband, the mayor — they had followed a court mandated schedule of joint custody for the dog — but Penelope decided now wasn't the time to talk about erasing women from history. No matter how hard she tried to fix society, most people referred to the mayor and forgot about his murdered ex-wife. Though maybe that had something to do with the mayor fleeing the country to avoid the police.

He laughed. "My last job was delivering pizza, and the mayor was on our banned list. One of the drivers refused to take an order out there, so my supervisor delivered it. Brutus knocked him down and ate the pizza and part of the box before anyone could stop him. Then the mayor griped about paying and didn't tip." Tick shook his head. "He was threatening to close the pizza parlor, but all the delivery places put his house on their banned list and he couldn't shut down everything."

"Brutus is a little better behaved now." Penelope was surprised to realize that was actually true. Mostly it was because they made sure he couldn't run out the door when food was delivered. He'd become accustomed to going into his crate when they were having anything brought over.

"I believe it. None of the kids got away with anything when you were in charge." At her raised eyebrows, he laughed again. "Not much, anyhow. You took all the fun out of it by trusting us to make our own decisions."

Penelope beamed. She'd been too busy earning enough money to keep up with the house payments so she didn't have to uproot her son. And Seth had always been an honest child. Her parenting approach had failed spectacularly a few times, but overall, she thought she'd done a good job.

Tick stood up and dusted off his hands. "But I do have to make you take the dog off the grounds. They're really strict about that here. Let me walk you out."

"Do you ever work in the mini drone kiosk?" The more information she extracted from Tick, the better, just in case Jake didn't get what he needed.

"Sometimes. Why?"

"Is there something that keeps the drones from flying over the neighborhood?" Penelope kept her steps slow, so she'd have enough time to ask all her questions. "I mean, there must be some people who try to leave the course, right?"

"Oh yeah, the first week we had them, people were buzzing their friends on the golf course, and a woman two streets away said there was a drone hovering outside her bedroom window. We almost got rid of them right away, but they added a feature to limit where they can go. The drone software doesn't let it fly outside the obstacle course."

They were almost at the gate. Penelope stopped and nudged Heidi toward the grass with her knee, pretending they'd stopped so the shepherd could sniff. Heidi stared up at her in confusion. "When we were here the other night, the drones were flying all over the golf course. Does the fencing software get turned off sometimes?"

"No, they just change the boundaries after dark." He glanced back at the pro shop.

Penelope figured she had time for one last question before he ran back to his boss. "There was a drone in a park over there on Sunday night." She gestured to the other side of the fence. With the opaque barriers surrounding the golf course, it was easy to forget the rest of the town existed. "How hard would it be to reprogram one of them to allow it to go over there?"

Now she had Tick's full attention again. "In the park? Couldn't have been one of ours. It's not like you can just redraw the boundaries — the company we bought the entire system from set up two software loads with the daytime and nighttime maps. Whoever's running the rental desk has to make sure the correct one is loaded." He winced. "Occasionally, if there's a big rush, the wrong version will go out, but at worst, someone could fly over the green in the daytime. They would never be able to fly to the park."

Penelope frowned at the fence. The drone had definitely been heading in this direction when she and Brutus had lost it. Had it stopped at a house somewhere in between? She and Jake had assumed it had to have been piloted by someone at the reception, but if they were wrong about that, the suspect pool opened up again. It could have been anyone.

Tick held out his arm toward the gate. "Ms. Standing? If you don't mind."

"Oh, right. Sorry." She walked to the exit, Heidi keeping pace next to her. "It was good to see you again. Tell your brother I said hello." Maybe Boom had gone back to his given name as well.

Outside the fence, she found a patch of green grass and sat down to wait for Jake. Heidi seemed disappointed at this continued delay, but settled next to her.

Both David and Kieran had been at the reception when Penelope and Jake had arrived, and she didn't think there had been enough time for either of them to have slipped out and come back unseen. Lenz couldn't have piloted the drone that picked up the blackmail money, and Penelope refused to believe Todd, Hannah, or Seth were involved.

Who else was left? That was their entire pool of suspects. Could the murdered cameraman, Sam Deu, have been working with one of them? Or, she supposed, the accomplice could have been someone else entirely. Except the crimes felt like they were being done by one person. She flopped back on the grass.

Heidi sniffed at her worriedly.

Jake spoke from the walkway. "Bored already?"

Just the sound of his voice made her feel better. "Depressed." She sat up. "The drones can't leave the grounds, which means we just proved the murderer can't be any of our suspects. We're back to where we started, except Todd's in jail and Hannah is a few days closer to giving birth." She frowned at his grin. "What?"

"Don't give up yet." He held out a hand to pull her to her feet. "We may have some evidence."

* * *

JAKE WAITED until they had crossed back to the park before explaining. "Maybe someone like Seth could figure out how to jailbreak the drones, but I don't think it could be done in the middle of a wedding reception without someone noticing." They settled into an easy stride that let them converse as they ran. "But there was an extra drone."

"How do you know that?"

"Because it's still there." They split apart to go around two women walking side by side, deep in conversation.

As they passed, Penelope heard one woman say, in the tones saved for the best gossip, "... hiding in their *closet*..." If she'd been on her own, Penelope would have stopped to tie her shoe or stretch so she could get a better sense of the conversation. Instead, she kept jogging and ignored the pang of never knowing what they were talking about.

Jake coughed. "If you want, I could fake a heart attack to make them stand around and finish the conversation where you could hear it." Clearly, he'd heard the same line she had, and he knew her well enough to guess her reaction.

Penelope grinned at him. "Have I mentioned how much I love you lately?" She shook her head. "Keep going. If I never find out who was hiding in someone's closet, it will just be one more thing I can blame on Todd."

Jake's bark of laughter made a woman sitting on the grass look up from her book. "Okay. The new one is the same make and model as the others, but the rental drones all have a number painted on the base and the controller. When Hector opened the booth on Sunday morning, there was an extra drone and controller without a number. It wasn't there Saturday afternoon when he clocked out, so sometime during the wedding reception, an extra drone appeared."

Letting the rhythm of their feet pounding the path provide a steady soundtrack, Penelope thought of how they could use this new information to prove who had done it.

"Fingerprints won't mean anything; everyone at the reception was trading controllers and helping each other get set up. Is it possible to track the purchase? They must sell hundreds of those things every day."

"Brianna's going to send someone to talk to the local vendors." At Penelope's confused glance, he explained. "I called her after I talked to Hector. The drone needs to be logged as evidence."

"You told her about the blackmail?"

"I... suggested there might be another aspect of the murder I couldn't talk about due to client confidentiality. She wasn't happy about it, but she understands. And when Lenz wakes up, he might be more willing to bring the police in now that someone tried to kill him."

Heidi perked up as they reached the far side of the park. Penelope handed her leash to Jake. "Don't hurt yourself. You're not fifteen anymore."

He merely gave her an impish grin and then sprinted away, the shepherd galloping by his side. Penelope watched them, their joy clear in their movements as they ran flat out around the perimeter of the park. The shepherd was faster, but not by much. This part of their joint runs had started one day when Penelope had needed to stop to talk to a client, and now it was the highlight of Heidi's day. Watching Jake move, Penelope hoped they would have the house to themselves sometime soon.

But since following that line of thought in a public park wasn't advisable, she stopped admiring his form and checked her mail. A potential client with a cat named Mittens had requested a meeting later that afternoon, which she confirmed and added to her schedule, and Seth had sent her another note. *Are you coming back for lunch? I might have found something.*

Penelope put her phone away and allowed herself a few

more seconds to admire both dog and man running toward her. Jake's face was shiny with sweat, but his smile was relaxed as he urged Heidi into one last burst of speed. They came to a halt next to her, both of them panting.

"I think we're improving."

"Like a fine wine. Or stinky cheese." She held up her phone. "Seth's awake."

Jake squinted, taking the phone from her so he could move it to the perfect distance from his eyes. He handed the phone back and then broke into a jog. "Looks like we have lunch plans."

CHAPTER 31

The kitchen smelled of fried eggs and ketchup, but Seth and Hannah were in the backyard talking while supervising Charlotte, who was playing catch with the dogs. Penelope watched from inside as the toddler wound up for a big throw. It fell two inches from her foot. Charlotte's belly laugh rang through the neighborhood. Brutus hit the ball with one paw, sending it flying into the bushes. Frodo ran in circles, barking, while the mastiff bounded through the plants.

Penelope winced. "We might need to get a few lavender plants at the nursery next week."

Behind her in the kitchen, Jake unscrewed the mayonnaise jar. "We might need to build a moat around the plants we want to live."

Turning from the scene, Penelope went back to the kitchen. "If that's what will make you happy. But you might want to think twice about intentionally giving Brutus a mud wallow every time it rains." She kissed Jake's cheek and took the plate he handed her, lifting the corner of the bread to check. "Ham, cheddar, pickles, *and* jalapeños? You really are a keeper."

"Just remember that the next time Brian and I do wood-working at two in the morning." He picked up his own more conventional ham sandwich and followed her to the table.

"The problem wasn't the power tools in the middle of the night. It was the six-pack of pale ale that preceded it."

Jake shrugged. "I have ten fingers. They can't all be important." His legs twined through hers under the table. Then he frowned at a paper with boxes and scribbles of text. "What does that say?"

Penelope leaned forward. "*About.* And *Promotional Packages.* I think Hannah must be designing her website." And it was Hannah's writing, she saw with approval, not Seth's. Now that she'd made the decision, Hannah was taking charge of her future. With any luck, she would be ready for her first clients as soon as she'd had a few months with the new baby.

The sliding door to the backyard opened, and chaos in the form of a toddler and two dogs poured in. Charlotte ran straight to Jake and raised her arms to be picked up. Now that the small child was no longer playing with them, the dogs focused on the table.

Clearing her throat, Penelope raised her eyebrows. Brutus flopped onto his bed in the corner of the kitchen. Then he had to stand up to let Frodo lie down in the middle. After the dogs were settled, Penelope went over and gave each one a treat. By the time she got back to her sandwich, Charlotte was curled up in Jake's lap, babbling nonsense syllables in tones that could be mistaken for complete sentences.

Jake widened his eyes as he looked at Charlotte. "Really?"

More babbling followed.

Still deep in conversation, Hannah and Seth wandered into the kitchen. "Once you pick a provider," Seth was saying,

"I'll set up the layout and you can fill in the ad copy whenever you're ready." He raised his head. "Oh, good, you guys are back. I need to show you something." He darted to the office and came back with his laptop.

When Charlotte pointed at the laptop with a serious face and spoke another nonsensical sentence, Jake nodded. "I agree. That's very important."

On the laptop's screen, the recorded meeting played. Seth pointed to one rectangle. "There's Kieran."

Penelope leaned closer so she could see the tiny window while the participants exchanged small talk. They seemed to be waiting for stragglers before starting. Behind the best man was a neatly kept hotel room, with patterned wallpaper and an impressionist print of a woman sitting in a field of poppies. The video stuttered, Kieran's voice lengthening and cutting out. On the screen, he fiddled with his phone, and then his voice came in clearly. "Sorry about that. The wifi at this hotel sucks."

Charlotte nodded solemnly and repeated his intonation. Hiding a smile, Jake tousled her hair.

Seth clicked on the video to pause it. "That's when Kieran dialed in through his phone."

Penelope squinted to see the nearly invisible earbuds. "You can do that?"

"Yep, that's pretty common, especially if your wifi is lagging." Seth sat back, realizing more explanation was needed. "Normally, both sound and video go through the computer, which is connected to wifi."

Penelope nodded. That fit her understanding of the world of technology.

Seth continued. "Meeting software always has another option for dialing in, usually so people who are driving can still connect. And if your wifi isn't good, using your phone will bypass it and talk directly to the cellphone tower, so the video will still be horrible, but at least you can listen and speak clearly."

Seth spoke with the air of someone who knew the system, so Penelope clamped down on her desire to ask why anyone would need to have so many meetings. There was a reason she had her own business, which required nothing in the way of bureaucracy other than the occasional text to Jake when he helped her out. "Okay, I've got it now."

After Seth tapped the space bar, the on-screen meeting continued. Kieran's image froze intermittently, but he answered questions. The video was hopelessly out of sync with the audio, which Penelope took as confirmation of the lagging hotel wifi.

This was nothing new — Penelope had let the video run in the background while she was reading the night before. "And then it continues for the next hour and a half. As far as I could tell, it doesn't loop. He's drinking water from a glass that gets progressively more empty. I don't see how he could have been somewhere else at the time."

By the look on Seth's face, there was a big revelation coming. "At the time of the recording, he was definitely in his hotel room." He paused dramatically. "But the time of the recording wasn't the time of the meeting."

Seth paused again, obviously waiting for everyone to congratulate him. Penelope glanced at Jake, who shook his head.

It was Hannah who understood first. "He recorded the video ahead of time!"

"But..." Talking to Seth about technology always made Penelope feel old. She let go of her irritation. "How? He's using the camera on his computer, isn't he?"

Seth nodded. "Sometime earlier, he recorded himself sitting in front of his computer. Then, after the meeting had started, he switched from the live webcam to the recorded video."

Penelope stared at him. "You can do that?"

"You'd need to download some software, but it's pretty easy. The steps are laid out online. Since Kieran was still on the phone contributing to the meeting, it looks like he sat there the entire time, but he could have been anywhere. All he needed to do was unmute his phone every once in a while, and he had an alibi."

Hannah looked around the table. "That's good, right? We can prove Kieran lied about where he was when the murder happened. That should be enough to get Todd out of jail, shouldn't it?"

After an uncomfortable moment of silence, Jake spoke. "We can prove Kieran *could* have lied about where he was. But that's different from proving he *did* lie. There's nothing here to prove he wasn't sitting in his hotel room like he said he was."

Tapping the side of the screen with his finger, Seth frowned. "The police should be able to look at his phone records to see if he changed cell towers during the call. But if I was going to do something like this, I'd use a burner phone. Or better yet, call in twice, once from the burner phone and once from my regular phone. Then I'd leave my regular phone behind at the hotel when I left."

Penelope was torn between pride that her son could plan a crime so thoroughly, and dismay that if Kieran murdered Ashley, he might be impossible to catch. "Would the meeting software people have a list of who called in?"

Seth shrugged. "Maybe?"

Jake helped Charlotte get down so she could go over to her mother. "I'll talk to Brianna."

Whether Brianna would or could follow up on that was another thing. The police had a good suspect already. Penelope scrolled the video back to the beginning. There had been something about Kieran's shirt... "Can you...?" She waved her fingers at the screen.

Seth broke in. "Mom, don't say *enhance*. It doesn't work like the movies. You can't make the picture better than the source."

"I know that." She did. Jake's heavy sighs every time the video was "enhanced" during detective shows would have told her, even if nothing else did. "I was going to say make it bigger," she lied. "There's something different about his shirt."

"Oh." Seth pulled his laptop closer and zoomed in. "Any bigger than this and the picture is just going to get grainier." He pushed it back to her.

Kieran's white dress shirt was slightly rumpled, either from the events of the day or from being packed in a suit-case. She scrolled forward to a later point in the meeting. Did it have fewer creases? She thought she might be imagining that, but *something* was different. She scrolled back and forth, trying to figure out what it was.

"Uh, Mom, can I...?" Seth took the computer away and worked for a few seconds, then slid it back to her. Now there were screenshots of two different times side by side.

"Oh, that's much easier. Thank you."

All four adults crowded around the laptop. Hannah bumped into Penelope and apologized. Then she added, "It's like those games where you try to pick out ten differences between two drawings."

"The light's a little different," Seth said doubtfully. "But not much."

Penelope wondered if it was time to break down and get reading glasses. But even with the image slightly blurry, she saw the difference she'd unconsciously noticed. "It's his collar. Look at it."

Seth nodded. "You're right. It's buttoned down here and not over here."

Angling the laptop so it faced her, Hannah looked more closely and nodded. "It's not the same shirt. See? He's wearing an Oxford button down collar here, and a dress shirt here. You can see the buttons on this one, but there aren't even button holes on the other."

Penelope decided she would have to take Hannah's word for that. She reminded herself there were many benefits to being in her fifties, and she wouldn't go back to her thirties for all the money in the world. Though she wouldn't mind having her thirty-year-old self's vision.

Warming to her subject, Hannah continued. "And the sheen of the fabric is different." She looked up to see them staring at her. "I worked retail during college. I spent half my time convincing guys going for their first interview that the OCBD was a bad choice. Oxford cloth button down," she clarified. "It's more casual than a dress shirt. Interviewers care."

"I showed up to my first interview in a retro Atari t-shirt and jeans," Seth commented.

"Programmers..." Hannah glanced over at him and shook her head. "*Some* interviewers care."

Turning so he could see everyone, Seth cocked his head. "Did we just solve a murder?" he asked in an awed voice.

Penelope met Jake's eyes. "Is that enough to get Todd off the hook?"

"Maybe. At the very least, it's proof that Kieran lied about his alibi. I'll take it to Brianna." His phone rang. He walked into the living room to answer it.

Penelope moved around the table to sit down, then stared at her empty plate. Had she finished her sandwich without noticing? Her stomach didn't feel full enough for that, but the dogs hadn't moved from their bed.

When she turned to look, Frodo was swallowing and Brutus was licking Charlotte's hands with gusto. Brutus regularly ate things that weren't even food, so she wasn't worried about him, but Frodo was an unknown quantity. Hopefully, his digestive system could handle cheese and jalapeños. If not, well... Cleaning up after a Chihuahua would be an order of magnitude easier than cleaning up after a mastiff. It was her own fault for forgetting the cardinal rule: never leave dogs or toddlers unsupervised.

Jake came back into the kitchen. "Lenz is awake. And he's well enough to talk to us."

CHAPTER 32

*P*ropped up in a hospital bed, dressed in a thin robe and connected to a variety of tubes and beeping medical devices, Lenz Russell retained the gravitas he projected on camera. Even the cowlick hadn't changed.

Penelope knocked on the frame of the open door. "You had us worried, but you're looking good." She set down the vase of flowers they'd brought from their garden to the array on the side table. Jake had said it was unnecessary to bring a get-well gift to a client, but Penelope argued that hospital rooms were too monotone to be comfortable. Mostly, she'd just wanted to get rid of a vase from the box in the garage. Every time someone sent flowers, she added another vase to the box, and it was overflowing.

"The police say they caught the guy." Lenz lifted a plastic straw to his lips, using the carefully controlled movements of someone trying to avoid pain. Then he grimaced. "Drinking tap water in a plastic cup might be worse than losing my spleen."

Penelope made sympathetic noises and let Jake take over the conversation. If she were in charge, she would feel obligated to start with how Lenz felt and then gradually transition to asking what they needed to know, but Jake — either due to his years in law enforcement, or just because men weren't encouraged to show feelings around other men — could plunge right in.

Jake proved her theory when he spoke. "We're not sure they have the right person. And if they don't, your life could still be in danger. You didn't see the driver, did you?"

Lenz shook his head. Then his breath hitched and he froze. "No. Just the car."

A nurse who could have been a model for a bodybuilding magazine came in and narrowed his eyes at Penelope and Jake. "Mr. Russell had major surgery, and he's not to tire himself."

"We'll keep it brief." Penelope smiled.

"Hmph." The nurse examined all the machines, writing notes on a clipboard. Then he turned and left, narrowing his eyes at Penelope on the way out.

Jake pulled his notepad out of his pocket. "Back when you attended that leadership course at Lone Pine College, did you ever meet a woman named Edie Glaspell?"

Lenz's eyebrows raised. "Lone Pine...? Oh. I'd almost forgotten about that. It was years ago." He blew out a long breath as he thought. "Edie? If I did, I don't remember." His voice smoothed out, as if he fell back on a rehearsed phrase. "Sorry, I meet a lot of people in my business."

"She was an English professor at the college, but rumor had it she was dating a student."

"Not me." Lenz's gaze unfocussed. "An English professor? There was... Oh, yeah, Kieran had a stack of poetry books in his room. Some girl he'd been hooking up with was super into it. But none of us ever met her. I thought she was a student taking classes over the summer."

Jake met Penelope's gaze. One more piece had fallen into

place, though Lenz's words were hardly proof. "Okay, we'll let you get some rest now." He turned, ready to leave.

Holding up a finger, Penelope said, "One last question." She moved closer to the bed and dropped her voice so none of the nursing staff would overhear if they walked by the room. "In Ashley's book, there's a part where the main characters sabotage a car, and it feels like it was something she witnessed." Edie's car had been sabotaged, but Ashley couldn't have been there to see it. There had to be another piece of the puzzle they didn't have yet.

Lenz's pale face took on an alarming gray tinge. "She *wrote* about that...?"

Only effort of will kept Penelope from rolling her eyes. *Men.* Lenz's close childhood friend had published a famous novel, and he'd never bothered to read it. Meanwhile, Penelope had struggled through an entire seven-volume self-published science fiction series just *because* the author was Seth's friend. "So it *was* written from something she'd seen."

Lenz's eyes closed, and for a moment, Penelope thought he'd gone to sleep. Or maybe died. But the machines kept beeping, and Lenz opened his eyes with the look of a man who had come to a decision. "We swore we'd never tell."

"We?"

"Kieran, Ashley and me." He sipped his water. "We were so young and all the adults agreed it didn't make any sense to ruin our futures. So it was just like it never happened. Sometimes I think I dreamed it."

Penelope reined in her frustration at his vague terms. "This was the summer before you all went to high school?" Esther had said something must have happened then, and she was right.

Surprise made his eyes turn toward her. "You know?"

"I have a pretty good idea." And she did, because the past had echoed into the future. "But I still need you to tell me."

He sighed. "Ashley never liked math. And that year, our math and science teacher picked on her. About the math, but everything else, too. Pointing out she had a hole in her shoe. Making fun of her handwriting when he knew she was dyslexic. Stuff like that." He drank again. "What we did was wrong, but Mr. Brewer was a bully who had no business teaching kids. Every day he singled her out."

"Her parents..." No, Ashley's father hadn't been in her life. "Her mother couldn't do anything?"

Lenz exhaled something that might have been a laugh. "That was the year her mother got into the whole 'free your mind by abandoning earthly possessions' thing. She would go on these 'spiritual retreats' for weeks at a time — I'm pretty sure they just dropped acid in the desert until they ran out of food. Whenever the electricity got shut off, Ashley would stay at my house." His voice dropped. "Kieran's parents thought she was a bad influence."

He fell silent. Though Penelope wanted to let him tell the story in his own time, she figured they had less than five minutes before the nurse came back and kicked them out. Plus, Lenz looked exhausted. "What happened that summer?"

His eyes flicked to her, as if he'd forgotten she was there. "Oh. Ashley failed math *and* science, so it was either summer school or she had to repeat the year. And Mr. Brewer was the summer school teacher. Instead of only having to deal with him for two periods, now she was stuck in his classroom all day. It was bad."

Penelope's heart broke a little for that twelve-year-old girl. Leaning back against Jake, she let his chest warm her back. "So the three of you decided to do something."

Lenz nodded once. "Or, I don't know. We never really came out and said, 'Let's kill Mr. Brewer.' It was more the three of us sitting around talking about how we wished his car would blow up or a meteor would crash into him. And then somehow that turned into us sneaking over to his house in the middle of the night and messing with his car. If it had just been me, I would have let the air out of his tires or loosened all the lug nuts or something. But Kieran made a hole in his brake lines and filled it with wax so it would be fine until he'd been driving a while."

"Where did he learn that?" At that age, Seth and his group of friends had spent their weekends running a complicated game involving orcs, wizards, and more dice than Penelope knew existed. She had worried he was so focused on this imaginary world he never went outdoors.

"Kieran's always been good with mechanical stuff. If he hadn't been so driven to get into politics, he would have made a good auto mechanic." Lenz's eyes drooped.

Rushing to finish before he fell asleep, Penelope said, "Mr. Brewer wasn't badly hurt." Even though Seth had gone to a different school, she would have heard if a teacher had been hurt or killed.

"No. The plan was stupid. Going from his house to the school, he didn't go over twenty-five miles per hour. Even if his brakes had failed completely, the crumple zone would have kept him safe. As it was, he took it to his mechanic and then the cops got involved and they figured it out pretty quickly. But since nobody got hurt... Our parents split us into different schools and we weren't supposed to see each other."

"And Mr. Brewer?" The fate of the teacher was incidental to the case, but Penelope needed to know.

Lenz roused himself enough to give a bitter smile. "Transferred to a different school district." Then his eyes closed and his face went slack.

Penelope tensed, but the machines kept beeping. Glancing over at Jake, she said, "He's just asleep, right?" Then Lenz took a breath and she relaxed. "What a mess."

Jake guided her out the door, his arm warm around her waist. "I need to talk to Brianna."

CHAPTER 33

*T*he afternoon dragged.

Penelope knew she was good at many things —
pet care, managing a complicated schedule, and picking
locks, to name a few — but nobody would have included
'waiting patiently' on that list. Jake had gone off to the diner
to explain their findings to Brianna, Seth was holed up in
Jake's office getting caught up on work, and Hannah and
Charlotte had gone to the park.

Before Jake had left, he had made Penelope swear she
wouldn't go anywhere near Kieran. "He thinks he's gotten
away with it all, but he knows you're asking questions."

Penelope lifted her right hand, thumb holding down her
pinky. "I promise."

Luckily, Penelope had a roster of pet sitting clients to
keep her busy. Evelyn Hofstetter hired her to let her corgi
puppy out, and that turned into a 45-minute game of fetch.
Mongo the Magnificent would have kept playing even
longer, but Penelope's shoulder hurt. "Tomorrow," she told
the eager puppy. Despite his attempts to get her to keep

throwing the ball, he settled quickly, burrowed in his blankets, and was asleep before she'd closed the door.

But just because she'd promised not to contact Kieran didn't mean she wasn't thinking about the case. The episode with Mr. Brewer had happened when they were kids. Edie Glaspell had died years ago. Why had Kieran killed Ashley *now*? Her book had already sold hundreds of thousands of copies — surely there was no point in killing Ashley to keep *that* quiet.

No. Something else had changed, something that had made bright, loyal Ashley a danger to Kieran after all this time.

Penelope jogged two blocks east to pull an arthritic husky around the block in his wagon. "We may have this backward," she told Fred as she always did, boosting his rear end into the cart. "Normally, it's the dog who pulls the sled." Instead of the short route around the familiar block, she pulled him to a different neighborhood so he could check out new smells. Every few houses, he climbed out so he could totter around and pee, letting the other dogs know he was still in charge, while Penelope checked her phone to see if there was any word from Jake. Then she helped the dog back into the cart and they moved further down the street.

As they crept along, the answer to the question of what had changed struck Penelope: blackmail. Kieran had blackmailed Lenz with the photos. And for the first time in years, Lenz had reached out to Ashley. Maybe the story of the stolen phone had been true. But how likely was it that Ashley hadn't sent those photos to Kieran that night? Kieran was fascinated by politics even then, and sending the pictures would have been a way of getting back at him for their fight. A sort of "see what you missed?" thing. No teenager would resist.

So Lenz told Ashley he was being blackmailed, and she'd been torn. Ashley had to have seen it was more likely that Kieran was behind it than some random person who'd found the phone. What would Ashley have done? Penelope knew what *she* would have done in Ashley's place: contact Kieran to make sure it wasn't him. But Ashley hadn't realized how much danger that put her in. She hadn't known Kieran had graduated to murder since high school — the death of an English professor at a tiny college would never make it to the New York papers.

Still no messages from Jake.

After Fred had been safely returned to his orthopedic bed with his favorite toys, Penelope scowled at her phone. How long could it take to lay out their evidence? She had one more appointment with the new client she'd added to the schedule that morning, and then she was going to stop pretending to be patient and call Jake. Or maybe go to the diner for some coffee and pie and accidentally run into them.

She checked the address and then the client's name. Remembering the name of a pet — in this case, Mittens the cat — was easy; keeping track of the owner's name took more effort. Sophia Grant. She repeated it twice until she was sure she'd remember it for at least the next fifteen minutes. The address given was the left half of the duplex over on State Street, right next door to Tinkerbell, the man-hating Rottweiler. Both sides of the duplex had been vacant for the last six months as the out-of-town owner tried to sell it.

"I keep telling him he has it priced too far above market value," Roselyn said when Penelope had asked the real estate agent about it two months earlier. "For that price, he needs to gut it and remodel, but he won't even replace the leaky hose in the front yard, so I can water the plants without making a mess." She had shrugged in resignation. "He might as well take it off the market and rent it out again. It's never going to sell this way."

The absent owner must have taken Roselyn's advice, or at least part of it. The For Sale sign still dominated the corner of the yard, with *Great Neighborhood* on a little placard hanging underneath. Everyone who had ever worked with Roselyn knew that sign meant she thought it was hopeless. *Motivated Owner* would mean the price was low, and *Great Interior* meant you might love it if you could overlook the outside. *Cute* meant it was small and well maintained.

But *Great Neighborhood* meant Roselyn couldn't find anything nice to say about the house itself. And even complimenting the neighborhood was a stretch, because this neighborhood included Tinkerbell. That might be a draw for the right buyer, but finding that person would take a bit of work.

When the ex-husband of Tinkerbell's owner broke into her house, Tinkerbell had sent him to the hospital and became a local hero. Praise for the dog had waned when a hapless gas technician had entered the yard for the semi-annual leak inspection. True, all Tinkerbell had done was growl menacingly. But the technician had been so frightened, he hadn't even been able to get his phone out to call for help. Now the house was plastered with so many warning signs it had become a new landmark for giving directions.

"Sophia Grant," Penelope muttered as she took the left fork on the walkway. The light in the doorbell button flickered, but she heard a tinny chime come from within.

A high-pitched voice called, "It's open!"

Penelope turned the dented knob, noting the cheap lock. It would take her less than thirty seconds to pick if she ever forgot her keys, but she supposed there was no point installing an expensive lock when the door frame looked like it would fall apart if someone leaned on it. She slipped inside, closing the door behind her so Mittens didn't get out.

The bare living room smelled of damp wood, incontinent dog, and bug spray. "Hello?"

"In the kitchen!"

Heading toward the source of the voice, Penelope walked across carpet worn so thin in places she could see the remnants of the compressed padding underneath. No wonder Rosalyn considered this listing a lost cause. "Doesn't look like you'll have to worry about your landlord taking your deposit if Mittens claws the carpet."

On the other side of the empty dining room, French doors made of a grid of tiny window panes showed the patchy grass and weeds of the backyard. Beyond the greenery was a five-foot pine fence, warped and drooping where the posts had rotted through. Penelope hoped the fence was replaced before any man tried to spend time in the backyard while Tinkerbell still lived next door.

Then she stepped onto the hideously patterned linoleum and came to a halt.

Kieran Engle stood two feet away.

CHAPTER 34

*P*enelope's body froze, but her mouth hadn't gotten the message. "*You're* not Sophia Grant." Betrayal flooded through her as she realized Sophia Grant didn't exist. She'd memorized that name for nothing.

"And there is no Mittens," Kieran agreed. He grabbed her upper arm when she took a step back. "Don't make this more difficult than it has to be."

Her pulse raced. "No promises." She could scream. The shoddy construction of the duplex wouldn't muffle her much, but she'd be competing with traffic noise and Tinkerbell's barking — nobody would hear her.

Kieran threw back his head and laughed, the sound bouncing off the stark surfaces of the dilapidated kitchen. "Oh, Ms. Standing, I do like you. It's too bad we couldn't have met under different circumstances." He snatched the phone from her hand and tossed it on the counter, where the scratched beige tiles contrasted strongly with the grout gone brown due to age and grime.

Penelope would have been just as happy if they'd never met in the first place. She pulled back, but his grip on her arm didn't let her move at all. "What does killing me gain?" If she got him talking, maybe he'd get distracted enough for her to get away.

He regarded her. "We do need to talk so I can find out where I went wrong. But let's do this first so we can both stop worrying." He reached into his back pocket with his free hand and pulled out a set of handcuffs. One end ratcheted closed around her wrist. He looked around the kitchen. "God, this place is a dump."

Penelope could see his point. Half the cabinet doors sagged, the linoleum was gouged and stained, and the faucet corroded. "We could go to the police station. It's a lot nicer there." She looked back at the living room. "How did you get in?"

"A friend lived here in high school, and I still had his spare key." He pulled her over to the refrigerator and clasped the other cuff around the door handle. "There. There's no way you're dragging this thing out of here."

Much as Penelope hated to admit it, he was right. Besides its weight, the refrigerator was probably welded to the linoleum by an accumulation of thirty years of spilled food and drink. No renter was going to bother moving a refrigerator to clean under it.

But if she had a few moments to herself and she could find a discarded paper clip or bobby pin, she could get out of the handcuffs; handcuff locks were much simpler than padlocks. Barring that, she thought she might be able to rip the folded metal handle out of one of its end brackets; there was a reason newer refrigerators didn't have one long piece of metal there.

However, both those choices required her to be unsupervised for at least a minute. She'd have to bide her time. "So, back to my question. What do you get out of killing me? I don't think you're the type of person who enjoys killing just for the sake of it."

"Of course not. But I can't have a career in politics with these murders hanging over my head, and I need another solid alibi to keep me in the clear."

Penelope couldn't help herself. "Because that worked so well when you murdered Ashley." It was one thing to be killed because she presented a danger, but losing her life so Kieran could try to fool the police again was unacceptable.

"I'll be in the police station giving a statement about where I was during Lenz's accident at the same time your body gets dumped. Or, at least, when your phone is still moving. They won't separate the two, and I'll be in the clear."

Kieran wouldn't have an accomplice — this had all started because he and Lenz and Ashley had done everything together. He would have learned that lesson. But moving something as light as a phone wouldn't require help. "What, are you going to pre-program a mini drone to carry my phone?"

From the look on his face, her guess had been correct. A flash of anger showed, and was quickly dismissed, just as it had been the night she'd cheated and won their contest.

Giving him a disappointed look, Penelope said, "It won't take Jake any longer than that to figure it out. The police already know. About the science teacher before high school, Mr. Brewer, and the woman in Lone Pine."

Penelope had forgotten her name again. Quickie Nicki? Why could she not remember that poor woman's name? No, wait, Speedy Edie. "Edie. And then Ashley. Because she put that scene in her book? Or because she figured out you were blackmailing Lenz?"

Kieran's brows drew down in confusion. "What does her book have to do with anything?"

"You didn't read it, did you?" It seemed unfair that Penelope had made it through seven typo-ridden volumes about two barbarians in space, Gh'xfut and Hqu'c'v, and Kieran couldn't be bothered to crack open the bestseller written by someone who had been a close friend. "I'm sure they'll have it in the prison library."

Shaking his head, Kieran said, "I thought she believed me when I said I'd deleted those photos years ago. But then she started telling people on that stupid group chat how the letter she was reading was going to air her deep, dark secrets." He shrugged. "Turned out she and Emma had a fling in high school, and she was going to read a love letter she'd written back then. But I didn't know that until she was already dead."

"It's too bad you couldn't have asked her first."

Kieran shrugged again. "It didn't matter. She'd started to suspect I was the one blackmailing Lenz, so she had to go." He narrowed his eyes at Penelope. "Don't give me that look. Lenz makes far more than he should with his ghoulish interviews, and I needed money to build momentum for a campaign. Once I get a seat on the state assembly, I'll be in a position to do a lot of good, and it only gets better from there."

Penelope tried to keep the disbelief off her face, but knew she wasn't successful. Kieran had killed three people, tried to kill two others, and now he was talking about how much good he would do? "Kieran, it's time to let me go and turn yourself in. There's not going to be any political career. The police know how you faked the video when Ashley was killed."

"They do not."

"Did you spill something on your shirt at the rehearsal? Is that why you changed it?"

He leaned against the counter. "One of the bridesmaids spilled red wine on my shoulder while we were waiting." He rolled his eyes. "I *should* have killed Emma's mother. The world would be a better place. That rehearsal was a disaster."

Penelope chose to ignore that. Bonding with Kieran by picking out people whom he should have murdered instead seemed like a bad idea. Even if she agreed with him a tiny bit. "Why Sam Deu?"

"Who? Oh, Lenz's camera guy? He saw me on the sidewalk that day, and he recognized me from the time Lenz did a feature on my boss. When he called, I thought he was going to shake me down."

Of course Kieran had thought that — he'd been blackmailing Lenz himself. "But he didn't." A roach scuttled from under the refrigerator and ran into the cabinet.

"No. He was working on a 'what did bystanders see' piece on his own. He was trying to prove his worth, so Lenz would bring him along when he took the new contract. Sometimes that go-getter attitude gets people killed. I couldn't let him live after that."

"And Lenz?"

He narrowed his eyes and pointed his index finger at her. "That one's on you. You asked about Lone Pine College, and I knew it was only a matter of time before you talked to Lenz."

Penelope tried to push a strand of hair behind her ear, only to have her hand yanked to a stop by the handcuff. "So... You didn't actually need to murder anyone this week. Ashley wasn't going to talk, Sam wasn't blackmailing you, and we had already figured out you were at Lone Pine for that leadership course before we talked to Lenz. That's a lot of crime for no purpose. I'm not sure I'd vote for you."

Kieran laughed. "I should have hired you to do my opposition research. Too bad."

Penelope kept a wary eye on two roaches crawling across the ceiling. "Even if the police didn't have any other evidence, you have to see how that video means you'll never hold political office." She finished in what Seth would call her "mom voice". "Unlock these handcuffs and we'll walk to the police station together. It's just a few blocks away. I'll make sure you get a decent lawyer if you don't already have one."

Something dropped onto her head. Penelope yelped and threw both hands up to pat at her hair. The handcuffs rattled as she yanked the link.

A roach bounced off her shoulder, fell to the ground, and scurried under the refrigerator. Penelope forced herself to ignore it so she could work on surviving this encounter.

Had she imagined the refrigerator handle shifting? Trying to make her movement casual, she pushed her shoulder against it. No, she hadn't imagined it. It definitely wiggled. Her jerking on it had loosened the bracket. Another good yank and it might come free.

But before she did that, she needed to figure out what to do afterward. The handle was lightweight — hitting Kieran with it might startle him, but it wouldn't knock him out or even slow him down much. On the off chance she made it out the front door, he'd grab her before she could get help.

But if she went out the *back* door, Tinkerbell would be just on the other side of the fence. The rotting wood would be easy enough to scale — but would she be fast enough? If she could get to the other side, Tinkerbell would protect her.

Kieran pursed his lips, considering. Then he shook his head. "Sorry, Ms. Standing. This could all still work out. I might as well go all in."

She could stay put and try to talk her way out of this. Or she could take this chance before Kieran noticed the loosened handle.

Penelope grabbed hold of the metal and *yanked*.

CHAPTER 35

*W*ith a twang of vibrating metal, the refrigerator handle came free. Penelope whirled and poked it at Kieran's head, wincing in anticipation when she got closer to his eyes than she'd planned. He ducked, giving Penelope enough space to run past him.

Kieran expected her to run out the front door, so when she turned toward the French doors leading to the backyard, it took him an extra moment to follow. For the first time, Penelope thought she might get away.

Kieran was fast.

He grabbed the back of her shirt, pulling her back, but Penelope had too much momentum. They crashed through the doors in a shower of glass and splintered wood. Penelope tripped on the door frame and went down, Kieran landing on top of her.

The fence was only five feet away, but it might as well have been five miles. Tinkerbell snarled, trapped on the other side of rotting wood and rusting nails.

When Penelope sucked in a breath, Kieran clapped his hand over her mouth, muffling her cry for help. It was unlikely that anyone had heard her. Even if they had, she didn't have ten minutes to wait for the police to appear.

Penelope struggled to roll out from under Kieran, hampered by the refrigerator handle trapped under her, keeping her from being able to raise one arm.

Glass crunched under her hips as she wiggled. Wood cracked. Penelope bit the flesh on the edge of Kieran's palm, gratified to hear him grunt in pain.

Then a low growl by her ear raised the hair on Penelope's neck. She and Kieran froze.

Turning her head slowly, Penelope saw two huge Rottweiler paws next to her. Tinkerbell had heard the commotion, and the fence hadn't held her back.

Kieran's whispered obscenity seemed appropriate for the occasion. Penelope held perfectly still — as far as she knew Tinkerbell only disliked men, but Penelope didn't want to confuse the dog.

The growl stopped as Tinkerbell inhaled, then came back, louder and scarier than ever. A line of drool slid to the ground.

Kieran fled. Pushing off Penelope's body, he scrambled through the remains of the French doors. The Rottweiler bounded after, chasing her prey. Inside the house, barking and snarling clashed with Kieran's screams.

Penelope carefully climbed to her feet, brushing off shards of glass. She stepped through the remains of the door and found her phone on the kitchen counter. In the living room, Kieran lay on the threadbare carpet, Tinkerbell standing on his chest.

"Help me! This dog is going to kill me!"

Kieran's forearm was held in Tinkerbell's mouth as blood dripped onto his shirt. Every time he moved, her growl got louder and he subsided.

Through the phone came the familiar voice of the dispatcher. "Nine one one, what's your emergency?"

Penelope took a long breath to steady her voice. "I need to report an attempted murder." Tinkerbell snarled louder. "And I think you should send an ambulance."

CHAPTER 36

By the time the police showed up, Tinkerbell had agreed to let Kieran huddle in the corner five feet away while Penelope crouched next to her and fed her treats. Not that it wasn't somewhat satisfying to see Kieran cowering underneath the enormous dog, but Penelope didn't want anyone to shoot Tinkerbell in the confusion. She made sure she had a good grip on Tinkerbell's pink collar before the first patrol officer burst into the room.

Once she was sure Kieran wasn't going to get away, Penelope retreated to the kitchen with the growling dog. Tinkerbell didn't distinguish between men in general and men in uniform.

Jake arrived a few minutes later. "Penelope! Has anyone seen my wife?" He stopped abruptly at the edge of the linoleum when Tinkerbell tensed and growled. Penelope scratched the dog's ears and gave her another treat, not loosening her own grip on the collar. "Hey, Jake's a nice guy," she murmured softly. "He's not going to hurt me."

Without changing her tone, she said, "Can you get me a leash and maybe clear everyone out of the house for a minute?" Tinkerbell had saved her life, but the Rottweiler was still amped up and Penelope didn't trust her to make good decisions about who might be dangerous. "Tinkerbell lives next door. I don't think anyone is home over there, but maybe you can find a leash."

"Are you...?" Jake wasn't bothering to hide his worry for her, even in a house full of cops. He took a deep breath. "I love you."

Penelope smiled up at him, eyes watering. "I love you, too. Now go find me a leash so Tinkerbell doesn't maul you when I give you a hug."

* * *

TWO HOURS LATER, Penelope was seated at Esther's table recounting the confrontation. Now that she had clean clothes, the only outward sign of her ordeal were a few small bandages covering glass cuts on her fingers.

After Penelope had finished giving her the details, Esther frowned. "It seems unfair to take the dog to jail. She deserves a medal."

Tinkerbell had been safely handed off to animal services — even though the bite had been entirely justified, legally the dog had to go through a 10-day rabies quarantine. "I know, but she gets to stay in a huge outdoor pen and the kennel workers know she's a hero. Last time, she gained five pounds from all the treats they were tossing to her. Besides, she needs to stay somewhere until the fence is rebuilt."

"Not by Red & Sons, I hope."

Penelope laughed. "No. Brian is flying in for the weekend. He and Jake are going to replace the whole thing." The two of them had built the Brutus-proof fence in her own yard, so she trusted the results. The safety of Tinkerbell and all the men in the neighborhood couldn't be left to Red & Sons, even if that *had* saved Penelope's life.

"Good." Esther poured more lemonade into Penelope's glass, even though she'd only drunk half of it. "I should have asked more questions when their parents split them up so intentionally right before high school. But I assumed it was either drugs or sex. It's a tricky time for parents."

Penelope nodded, remembering those days. Seth had never gotten into any serious trouble, but she'd still worried about every decision she'd made.

Would Kieran have turned out differently if things had been handled better when they'd tried to kill the science teacher? Possibly. Penelope didn't believe incarceration helped most people, much less young offenders. Counseling might have been a good place to start, though. Ashley Webb might have been allowed to mature and write more books. Sam Deu's enthusiasm might have gotten him the dream job.

On the other hand, Kieran might have gone to a juvenile detention facility, met willing accomplices, and learned how to hide his crimes better. It was impossible to know for sure.

Penelope checked the time and stood. "I have to go. They should be just about done releasing Todd. Jake's picking him up and we're all going to have dinner together before everyone goes home."

Esther looked up with a straight face, though her eyes twinkled. "And how is Todd doing?"

Sighing, Penelope rolled her eyes. "Who knows? Maybe this whole thing will be the kick in the pants he needs to realize what a good thing he has with Hannah." She thought about the fire in Hannah's eyes when she talked about running her own business. "But I think Hannah will be alright no matter what happens."

"Good for her." Esther rolled to the counter and picked up a paper plate with yellow cellophane bundled around it. "I made ginger cookies. Tell Hannah to eat a few when she's ready to jumpstart her labor. They should keep until then."

The cellophane crinkled as Penelope took the plate. "Does that really work?" A lifetime ago, when she'd been pregnant with Seth, she'd heard enough quasi-facts on how to induce labor to fill a book. Spicy foods, eggplant, pineapple, cupcakes... If something could be eaten or drunk, it was on the list. Anyone desperate enough to drink a tablespoon of balsamic vinegar was likely overdue — at some point labor would start even if they did nothing at all.

"Probably not." Esther headed for the front door to see Penelope out. "But it will help her feel like she has some control over it all. That's worth a little white lie." They went out onto the porch. "Try not to kill Todd. Those poor detectives already worked all weekend."

* * *

DINNER WAS PIZZA, ordered from Seth's favorite restaurant. In a fit of magnanimity, Penelope ordered a small single-topping pizza for Todd, though she wondered how she'd ever thought she would spend the rest of her life with someone who insisted on a plain mushroom pizza every time.

Despite having showered and changed into clean clothes, Todd seemed different as he sat on the couch next to his daughter. He'd even thanked Penelope for ordering the pizza, which was new. Usually, he just assumed the things he wanted showed up on their own and complained if they weren't there. Now he wasn't even grumbling about Brutus lying on his feet and gazing longingly at Todd's food.

Hannah picked off green peppers from her daughter's pizza, putting them on her own plate. "And the dog really knocked down a fence to save you?"

"She did!" Penelope didn't voice her other theory, that the

rotting boards had disintegrated when the Rottweiler leaned on them. Tinkerbell deserved to be the hero of the story. "She must have heard me yell for help."

Seth shuffled the pizza boxes on the coffee table. "Anyone want the last sausage? I wish I could have seen Kieran's face when the dog started growling."

Hannah gave Charlotte her plate back. "There you go. No more peppers." She licked sauce off her fingers. "You're much braver than I am. If a roach fell off the ceiling onto my head, I'm pretty sure I'd just scream until I passed out." She shuddered. "Getting kidnapped and handcuffed is horrible, but the roaches..." She squeezed her eyes shut and shivered.

Penelope laughed from her spot on the floor next to Jake. "I'm with you. But if it hadn't fallen on my head, I never would have jerked away so hard, and I'd probably still be stuck." She turned to look at her husband. "I need to practice picking handcuffs."

Todd stared at her in disbelief, but Jake leaned in to kiss her temple. "I'll borrow a pair for you to work on."

CHAPTER 37

*T*odd still looked unsettled when they all went out to load up the minivan thirty minutes later. Jake and Seth were repacking everything to make it all fit, and Hannah was strapping Charlotte into her car seat.

Hanging back so they wouldn't be overheard, Todd took a sharp breath. "Thanks for taking care of Hannah and Charlotte and... everything."

Penelope really wanted to console him on how much that speech must have hurt, but decided it was time to act like an adult — just this once. "You're welcome. Hannah is amazing, and I'm ready to keep Charlotte here forever." She met his gaze. "Don't mess this up. They can definitely manage without you, but this is probably the last chance you'll ever get to have a real family. Don't blow it."

Instead of arguing with her as she'd expected, Todd cast a worried glance at the minivan. "It might be too late."

Penelope narrowed her eyes at him. "She stayed at her husband's ex-wife's house for two days so she could help get you out of jail. That's not how someone acts when she's already given up on her marriage."

A faint, rueful grin played over his features. "Not what you would have done?"

"If I'd driven my pregnant self all the way here with a toddler in the back and seen you in front of some other woman's house, I would have run you down without a second thought." She socked his shoulder lightly. "You're an idiot if you don't spend the rest of your life showing Hannah that you can change for the better."

He glanced back at the minivan, this time more hopefully. "You know, I hate it when you're right."

They shared a genuine smile, possibly the first since Seth had been a small child.

Hannah's goodbye was quicker because Charlotte was already complaining about being restrained. "Thank you so much," she said, hugging Penelope as tightly as she could, considering the bulk of the bump between them. "I don't know how I would have survived this without you."

"Any time. I mean it." Penelope stepped back so Hannah could climb into the passenger seat. "Call me if you ever just need to talk to an adult for a while." Next to her, Jake cleared his throat, but his face was innocent when she turned her head to look.

They stood on the curb and waved as the minivan drove away. Seth sighed. "I have to get back home. Thanks for letting me spend the weekend."

Penelope hugged him. "You're always welcome."

Seth tossed his overnight bag into the middle of the empty energy drink cans and fast food wrappers in the back seat of his car. When Seth started the engine, Penelope took Jake's hand. "You can say it now. He can't hear you." She'd heard the noise he'd tried to stifle at the sight of the mess.

"I have no idea what you're talking about."

She waved to Seth and leaned back against Jake's chest, pulling his arms around her. "I love you."

His hug tightened. "I love you, too."

* * *

BACK INSIDE, settled on the couch in their customary positions with the drone of professional golf on the television, Penelope took Jake's hand. "After all those people being here all weekend, it feels kind of empty now." Brutus yawned and adjusted the position of his head on her feet.

"Empty in a good way?"

"Just different." She let her mind wander, then sat up. "We should make sure Lenz knows Kieran was arrested, so he doesn't worry about someone showing up at the hospital to finish him off."

Jake huffed a laugh. "You're hours too late. Lenz called while you were in the shower. He got the job with the national news. From what I could tell, it was *because* of all this, not in spite of it. And while he's recovering, he'll be working on a segment about growing up with a serial killer."

Penelope turned to look at his face to see if he was serious. "Already?" She snuggled back against his shoulder. "I guess I shouldn't be surprised. Lenz has never let good taste impede his career."

"That sums it up pretty well. Oh, and they finally reached Ashley's mother. She and her group will be in town in a few days. They're not staying here," he added hurriedly.

Penelope reached back to pet the chihuahua, who had taken his usual place on the back of the couch. "Is she going to take Frodo?"

"Brianna didn't say."

The living arrangements of the dog wouldn't be important when telling a woman her daughter had died. "I've gotten used to having him here. Maybe she won't want to bring a dog on the road with her."

"He's not the worst dog ever," Jake agreed.

On the television, a ball arced up and away, accompanied by a chorus of oohs and polite clapping. Penelope smiled. "The house *is* finally empty."

"That sounds like my cue." Jake leaned over to kiss her, then froze at Frodo's snarl. "Or maybe Ashley's mother has been wanting a little dog for years."

Penelope laughed and slid off the couch. "Must be time to take this upstairs. I'll get the dogs their treats while you lock up."

They walked to the kitchen hand in hand.

* * *

I HOPE *you enjoyed Penelope's latest adventures! Turn the page for a preview of* The Penelope Standing Mysteries *holiday novella.*

If you would like to be notified of new releases, as well as receive exclusive short stories and other bonus content, join my free newsletter at https://tmbaumgartner.com/subscribe/.

DEATH TRIMS THE TREE (PREVIEW)

(A cozy holiday novella about missing ornaments, lucky cookies, and the joy of family and friends!)

DEATH TRIMS THE TREE (PREVIEW)

(A cozy holiday novella about missing ornaments, lucky cookies, and the joy of family and friends!)

CHAPTER 1

*D*espite fifty years of trying, Penelope still couldn't wrap a present to save her life.

Spiced cider bubbled on the stove, filling Esther's kitchen with the scents of cinnamon, cloves, and apple. It was a combination Penelope normally loved. Today, though, it just reminded her of the air freshener one of her pet sitting clients had sprayed around their foyer yesterday. Instead of covering up the smell of moldy carpet, the spray had linked all the scents in a way Penelope was hoping to forget.

Tchaikovsky's Nutcracker Suite played on the speaker mounted in the corner. For some reason, it seemed to Penelope like the soundtrack of a heist movie more than anything else. Still. Better a heist movie than the endless repetition of novelty Christmas songs in the stores over the last two months.

There were four days until Christmas, and she really wasn't in a holiday mood.

The stacks of gifts still needing to be wrapped extended all the way to the front door, leaving barely enough room for Esther's wheelchair to get through. When two of her friends had needed to drop out of Santa Sleighs — a truly unfortunate name for such a worthwhile charity — Esther had offered to take over. So now she was decorating gifts for twelve families in town instead of four. Even the cats had been temporarily banished to their room to keep the production line moving.

At the kitchen table strewn with wrapping supplies, Penelope folded the end paper into a triangle on both sides, lifted the resulting trapezoid, and secured it with clear tape. The edges gaped, so she taped those down as well, then added another piece at the top just in case it got any ideas about letting loose. After all that, she affixed the tag with the recipient's name and added the final result to the stack with all the others.

Nobody would have any difficulty figuring out which of these presents she had wrapped. Esther's corners looked like corners, not the art project of a five-year-old. Maybe in another thirty years or so, Penelope would be as good as Esther, but she doubted it.

Esther caught her staring at the packages. "Relax. The children won't care if Santa looks like he had a few too many before he wrapped their presents." She placed another neatly wrapped book on top of the pile. "Since when have you developed a streak of perfectionism?"

The idea startled a laugh out of Penelope, despite her mood. "Can you imagine? I'd never get anything done." She picked up the next toy, a robot that converted into a train. "I'm fine. It's just going to be the first Christmas Seth hasn't been able to stop by, and I'm feeling sorry for myself." Her son was in his thirties and was doing well. She was excited about his trip to New Zealand; she just wished he could somehow clone himself so he'd be in this hemisphere for the holiday as well. "Part of the problem is I've been conditioned by all the songs and movies to expect snow and cold weather.

Not that it ever snows *here*, but normally it's a little colder than this. And then Seth keeps sending pictures where everyone is in shorts and relaxing in the shade. It's messing with my brain."

The box for the train robot had three different sections for the body and a rounded top, and would have been a challenge for anyone. Penelope decided she wasn't going to feel bad about how this one turned out. She cut off a big section of the red paper decorated with green kittens chasing golden bows.

"It might get below freezing tonight. Maybe that will help. How goes the great Christmas present hunt?" Esther asked.

Penelope and her husband had made a pact not to buy Christmas gifts for each other this year, which had sounded like a great idea in October, but had led to increasing desperation as the holiday approached.

Penelope sat up straighter. "I looked through a bunch of boxes last night, and I think I've figured it out. Jake once talked about this dessert his aunt brought by every year. One of those things that might be an acquired taste but makes the holiday real for you."

Esther nodded as she used her scissors to slice off a square of the green paper with red puppies. "Like my father's challah." She smiled as she situated four skeins of yarn on the table. "He added candied orange peel and chunks of fig, which always threw off new people. But that's what I grew up with, so I've always made a loaf that way for special holidays."

Penelope wrapped the paper over the top of the robot, but that left a bare spot near the side. Taping the side together, she cut off another piece of paper to cover the gap. "Anyhow, I found the recipe. It's some sort of English Christmas pudding. It's supposed to be made a month in advance, but a few days is going to have to do. I just need to figure out how to keep him out of the house for six hours while it steams. Or else just admit that's what I'm doing and ruin the surprise."

"Make it here." Esther gestured at her stove. "I can keep an eye on it while you're off walking dogs."

"Thank you." Penelope leaned back and eyed the robot. Perhaps if she added some ribbon, it would look better. "Would tomorrow work?"

"Tomorrow would be fine. I'll be here wrapping gifts for the toy drive in any case." Esther finished yet another neatly wrapped gift and added it to the stack. "Now that the important things are out of the way, tell me about what Jake is doing. I heard Linda Schmidt hired him to track down a rolling pin."

Esther's description made Penelope smile. "It's not just a rolling pin. It's an antique that makes a special pattern on cookies. Her great-grandmother brought it with her when she emigrated from Germany way back when. Eating cookies made with it provides good luck for the year."

Esther gave her a dubious look.

Penelope nodded. "One year her great-grandfather insisted his wife only make 'American' treats so she used the rolling pin in secret and he didn't get any of those cookies. Then he died two months later." From other details, Penelope suspected someone should have checked the corpse for strychnine, but everyone involved was dead now, so it probably didn't matter. "And one time Linda's aunt went on a cruise and didn't bake cookies, and that was the year her husband left her for the housekeeper and won the lottery right after the divorce was finalized."

Esther snorted. "Bad luck, indeed."

Penelope nodded. "So nobody wants to tempt fate. Linda and her cousins share custody of the rolling pin. Whoever has it makes cookies for everyone. This year it was Linda's turn to have it, and it disappeared from her porch before she got home." She loosened the ribbon so it didn't look like the robot was being strangled.

Esther glanced at the spool of ribbon still in Penelope's hand and then dug out another one from the bag of supplies. "I thought maybe it was one of those ridiculously expensive things some cooking show was touting. Though now that I think of it, that doesn't seem like something Linda would buy." Esther sighed. "People are driven to crime for understandable reasons, but I do wish there was some way to protect things that only have sentimental value."

Penelope nodded, though she wasn't quite as convinced as Esther of the general innocence of humanity. Sometimes people were just jerks. "At least stealing packages makes more sense than holiday decorations. The Gundersons decorated the pine tree in their front yard two nights ago, and today, all the ornaments and garland are gone. And Liz Loewecki had a wreath on her front gate wander off. Who takes that sort of thing? You can't possibly resell that."

A tiny piece of tape was all Esther needed to anchor the paper on her next present. "Someone trying to make the neighborhood more tasteful? Though if that were the case, they would have started with Drew Franklin's house."

Penelope had been by the house the day before and agreed with Esther. Drew Franklin, or Pastor Franklin, as he insisted people call him, projected a short video onto the side of his garage to remind people of "the reason for the season." That scene was followed by an exhortation for women to be more modest, with the tagline "Be like Mary — chaste, not chased!"

In what had perhaps *not* been the most mature response, Penelope had uttered a choice phrase and lifted her shirt to flash the house. Not that there was much to see — she'd been wearing a sports bra underneath. It had still made her feel better.

In Esther's kitchen, she grinned at the memory. "I'm tempted to go by that place with a bunch of water balloons. I'm pretty sure that equipment isn't meant to be left outside in the rain."

Esther's fingers didn't slow at her task. "Just let me know ahead of time so I can make sure you have a solid alibi."

Friends like Esther made the world a much better place. "Back to the rolling pin. It sounds like most of the package thefts are happening in one area, so Jake is on a stakeout."

Now that he was no longer with the police, her husband could only note down the license plate and follow the car to its destination, but he still had a few detectives in the department on speed dial. If Jake could find the person stealing packages, the department would have a patrol car at the house before the items could be sold.

Esther folded a bit of ribbon into a symmetric bow and taped it on another package. Penelope evaluated her own creation. With the ribbon draped around the problem area, the robot now looked like it had been wrapped by a drunk and given a feather boa as a consolation prize. She gave up and moved on. For the next present, she chose a puzzle in a sturdy box.

Esther transferred the wrapped presents off the table into a large gift bag. "How bored is he?"

Penelope rocked one hand back and forth. "He brought Brutus along in the car for company, and he's taking regular training breaks. But he's also called me seven times since yesterday at noon, so..."

"So, moderately bored," Esther said.

"Yep." With the puzzle quickly wrapped and the robot no longer in evidence, Penelope decided she liked wrapping the toys that were more of a challenge. "I offered to swap with him for a while, but he seemed to think I might confront the thief instead of letting the police arrest them. I have no idea why he would think that."

Esther refused to meet her eyes.

Penelope shook her head. "Anyway... If he wants to be on the phone while I'm jogging with a dog, that's fine. Not the sort of heavy breathing phone calls some couples have, but you know how it is. We're getting older."

Esther snorted. "I've seen the way you look at each other."

Penelope checked her phone. "I need to get going." She cleaned up the stray bits of wrapping paper and ribbon in front of her. "I'll be back tomorrow with Christmas pudding ingredients, so if you haven't finished by then and you still want me to help, I can wrap a few more after I finish mixing in the kitchen."

Esther nodded. "Tell your young man he's welcome to come over to help if he gets bored in the car today."

"Don't tempt him." Penelope headed out, passing the neatly stacked presents and wondering how many Esther had bought on her own. "He needs to finish this case so I don't have to join him on the stakeout in order to exchange gifts. I'd rather not heat up a Christmas pudding on the radiator if at all possible."

Esther laughed. "No promises."

* * *

READY FOR MORE? Get Death Trims the Tree from your favorite retailer now!

ACKNOWLEDGMENTS

I had a great time writing this book, but it never would have happened without my writing and critique partners. Every single one of you is awesome, even if you make fun of my comma usage.

And my ARC readers! I'm still have trouble believing how lucky I am — people are willing to read *and* review my books. I feel like a real author now! Thank you so much!

Once again, my brother Eric has gone on a typo hunt. He also tries to keep me consistent in spelling all those words which have alternate spellings I've internalized after a lifetime of reading British mysteries. (Seriously, though, can we not just pick either *gray* or *grey*? I don't even care which one we choose!) (Eric cares, though. He makes me use *gray*.) Anyhow, he deserves a round of applause. And maybe a new grey t-shirt.

ABOUT THE AUTHOR

Tess Baytree is the pen name of speculative fiction author T. M. Baumgartner. At various times she has been a veterinarian, Unix system administrator, software developer, and after-hours book-shelver in a medical library.

Theresa currently lives in Northern California in a house with too many animals. She knits hats for garden gnomes and runs with scissors only when absolutely necessary.

Want updates about new releases? Silly dog anecdotes? Join the newsletter mailing list! Go to https://tmbaumgart ner.com/subscribe/ or point your phone's camera at the QR code above.

ALSO BY TESS BAYTREE